THE SE
CONFESSION

By

Sven Hughes

For Olga.

CONTENTS

ACKNOWLEDGEMENTS.. i

Chapter One.. *1*

Chapter Two *8*

Chapter Three *18*

Chapter Four *23*

Chapter Five *27*

Chapter Six *30*

Chapter Seven... *37*

Chapter Eight *41*

Chapter Nine... *44*

Chapter Ten.. *48*

Chapter Eleven.. *63*

Chapter Twelve.. *66*

Chapter Thirteen *68*

Chapter Fourteen... *82*

Chapter Fifteen.. *86*

Chapter Sixteen... *98*

Chapter Seventeen... *103*

Chapter Eighteen... *118*

Chapter Nineteen *131*

Chapter Twenty... *134*

Chapter Twenty-One *147*

Chapter Twenty-Two *154*

Chapter Twenty-Three *161*

Chapter Twenty-Four... *169*

Chapter Twenty-Five.. *175*

Chapter Twenty-Six.. *180*

Chapter Twenty-Seven *191*

Chapter Twenty-Eight.. *196*

Chapter Twenty-Nine..*207*
Chapter Thirty *215*
Chapter Thirty-One..*218*
Chapter Thirty-Two *221*
Chapter Thirty-Three *232*
Chapter Thirty-Four..*235*
Chapter Thirty-Five...*238*
Chapter Thirty-Six *243*
Chapter Thirty-Seven...*249*
Chapter Thirty-Eight *255*
Chapter Thirty-Nine *260*
Chapter Forty..*269*
Chapter Forty-One *296*
Chapter Forty-Two...*301*
ABOUT THE AUTHOR 303

ACKNOWLEDGEMENTS

The completion of any book requires the help of a flight of angels. With this in mind, I would like to thank:

- The broadcaster Bob Mills, who has been my confidant, adviser, and unfailing supporter through every chapter of this endeavour.

- Svetlana Sorokina-Wilson and Elena Davies, for the brilliance of their notes and comments.

- Rebecca de Vere and the entire team at Bury Hill Fisheries in Surrey, for their patience in the face of so many questions.

- My agent, Jo Bell, at Bell Lomax Moreton, for pushing me further at every opportunity.

"You can't imagine how stupid the whole world has grown nowadays."
– Nikolai Gogol, Dead Souls

Chapter One

It's as if the garden has been designed for her specific purpose. Cash to enter, gloves permitted, no CCTV coverage and a small guidebook to help her locate the exact specimens.

There are only three other visitors this morning, on account of the unseasonably cold autumn weather: a Filipino nanny resentfully pushing an expensive pram, a tight-faced septuagenarian striding determinedly for the benefit of her smartwatch, and a forlorn man in his forties lost in his life's disappointments. Nonetheless, she completes a thorough circuit of the grounds, alert to any unwanted disciples, before homing in on her objective.

She is in her early forties, taller than average and with a swimmer's physique: broad shoulders resulting from perspiration, rather than genetics, a lined forehead from frowning, rather than laughter and a brusque manner born of professional need. Her body is her business.

There, just in front of the Propagation Glasshouse, is the drab border, adorned with its own weathered information board: *Plants cannot move to escape their predators, so they have developed poisons…'*

She's not the first to use the Chelsea Physic Garden as a clandestine larder. Since its founding in 1673, these three-and-a-half acres, tucked away behind high red-brick walls in the centre of London, have supplied countless furtive slayers, as well as apothecaries, most notably the Bulgarian Secret Service, which sourced *Ricinus communis* from this very border for their assassination of Georgi Markov.

She surveys the end-of-season offerings. The leaves on the large *Atropa belladonna* have started to curl at their edges, revealing a glistening constellation of aubergine berries. Their lethal succulence is tempting, but she has another method in mind. She continues on her travels, past the *Myrrhis odorata* of Central Europe and the *Lathyrus sativus* of Southwest and Central Asia, before returning closer to home in favour of *Oenanthe crocata*, a prolific native.

Whether referred to as *Hemlock Water-Dropwort*, *Dead Man's Fingers* or *Dead Tongue*, the result is always the same: a constriction of the muscles resulting in asphyxia, coupled with a taught rictus grin on the face of the deceased. On this occasion, the client has insisted that he wants this macabre last leer as part of the deal. "It's a need to have, not a nice to have." A prerequisite for the full settlement of her invoice.

*

His brief to her had been notably old-school in its

manner. A set of printed instructions from a masked courier, comprising an address, date and check-in details, as well as an oblique reference to her standard fees having been acknowledged and accepted. An anonymous hotel near Heathrow airport with plenty of footfall. A booking made for her in an assumed name. On entering the room, a plastic pedestal chair in front of – but at a suitable distance from – the aptly named *communicating* door to the adjacent room: vintage tradecraft that indicated a client who didn't trust the claims of the supposedly secure new technologies.

Sitting, facing the opposite wall, as per her instructions, she had waited in the classic *ready* position: relaxed hands on her lap, feet beneath her centre of gravity. Just in case. Finally, there was a slight rush of air from behind her that heralded the opening of the partition door and a chlorine-tingle in her nose from the bleach-filled bucket that the client had placed to cloak their scent, and thus their sex. Then, the low-pitched whisper, scrambled by a voice-altering device, outlining the task and specifying the need for the target's last leer. Finally, the dossier left on the floor beside the now-closed communicating door. No surprises. No need to reach for the weapon discreetly holstered beneath her belt buckle. Just a textbook brief for a standard *wetwork* mission. She was in and out within twenty minutes.

*

She harvests the stem and leaves, being sure to avoid the staining yellow liquid that oozes from each incision. The sweet smell of the foliage reminds her of parsley. She will mash and brew her preparation back at the bed-and-breakfast this evening, then make her way to the kill zone in the morning, using the rush-hour commuters for cover. No name, just a photo in the briefing dossier. Male. Sixties. Heavy-set, with a Father Christmas beard and thick horn-rimmed glasses. A location and a time. She will be there, waiting.

*

He arrives, as anticipated, just before nine. A morning routine that has been meticulously documented by another hand. By a former spook most likely, now selling pattern-of-life reports on the commercial market. Every aspect of the target's diary and comportment surveilled and noted, except for his name and profession. He remains anonymous: simply a target. The dossier a freshly primed canvas on which she will now paint his final moments. He orders black tea, with lemon. She detects an accent. Eastern European. Polish perhaps. He then takes his regular table near the centre of the room and opens his paper at the international pages. All foreseen.

From her corner table, she uses the reflection in the café's large glass frontage to fully confirm his identity. The brown eyes unusually accentuated by the cheap glasses. The manicured nails, the right hand more finished than the left, confirming that he is left-handed. The blunt jawline and steep forehead. She has her man. From this angle, she can even see what he is reading: an article about some new peace accord between Russia and one of its former territories. She savours the intimacy. Two reflections united momentarily in the window glass. Two lives coexisting in a single pane and plane, although passing in opposite directions: one thrusting forward determinedly, the other about to wind down towards its unsuspecting end. The exchange of energy already underway. Entropy embalmed within the glassy surface. She finishes her coffee and discreetly wipes the cup and table of prints with a paper serviette.

*

The toxins won't take immediate effect. She has time to pick up the pair of light blue trainers she saw in the window of the neighbouring shop, which was still closed when she entered the café. By the time he is feeling short of breath, she will already be lost among the late commuters and early shoppers. As he makes his way to the café's toilets or, having made his excuses, to the street in search of fresh air, she will be changing trains, deep underground. Next, he will recount his recent meals, in search of the cause of the presumed food poisoning, and she will be switching trains for a second time. Only when she re-emerges into the cold morning sun on the other side of London, will the reality of his predicament have finally hit him, along with the full force of the *Oenanthe crocata*. He will be unable to communicate his revelation to others, as his entire effort will be focused on the simple act of breathing. Desperate, he will gesticulate for help, grasping at strangers, then fall at their feet, clasping his throat, precipitating a call to the emergency services, who will arrive too late to save him. She will then pick up her daughter from the drop-in nursery and accept the doubtless compliments for her new blue shoes, and he will be dead, grinning from ear to ear.

*

She gets up from her table and crosses to the door. He doesn't look up from his paper as she slips the bright yellow pellet of distilled pulp into his cup. The colour variance of his tea is marginal; the pellet blending unobtrusively with the lemon-infused liquid. It is this attention to detail that sets her pricing. "You're paying for peace of mind," as she used to have to tell prospective clients. But now her reputation precedes her, and her prices are non-negotiable.

*

One last look back from the doorway to confirm that the target is indeed drinking the infusion. He will remain there, reading his paper, for another thirty minutes, as he does every morning. Then he will get up, fold his paper under his right arm, and having left a tip, begin his day. Today, his final day. She exits the café and turns right, towards the shoe shop.

Chapter Two

Wearing her dazzling new blue trainers, she turns for the station. Her mind has already moved on from the job. She left that manifestation of herself in the café, along with her poison, and in the shop, along with her old shoes. She is now just another morning traveller, bustling through her chores, to the distant register of a nursery's escalating fees.

It is then that she sees him. The target. Crossing the street ahead of her. No newspaper now, but with a mobile phone pressed to his ear. It can't be. But there he is, striding in rude health and with a clear purpose. Her disconcertion is not a fear of failure. She saw him drink, and with so little time having elapsed, the toxin's more pronounced effects are not to be expected so soon. Instead, her sense of disquiet relates to his sudden change of routine. This is entirely at odds with his pattern-of-life dossier: a man of such entrenched early-morning habits. Intrigued, she follows at a discreet distance. Her alibi is anyway-sound as they are heading in the direction of the station.

He walks for a further few minutes, only pausing once to remove a handkerchief from his pocket and mop his brow. Evidence of exertion, or the start of the physiological effects. She cannot be sure from this distance. She would need to see his eyes – the contraction of his pupils – to confirm the latter.

Now he is waving, as he simultaneously pockets his phone. He is approaching a second man, who is waiting, holding open the front door to a private residence wedged between two shops. The stranger is younger, lither, with a sharp face and something of the wolf about him. A warm handshake between the two develops into a brief hug, then the wolf ushers the target ahead of him, up some carpeted stairs just visible through the doorway as she passes. The door closes behind them.

*

She should go now. Whatever the reason for the target's unexpected behaviour, it is no concern of hers. She has administered the pellet, without suspicion, and the dosage is sufficient to ensure lethality as well as the all-important smile that will release her payment. Her work is done. But she doesn't go. Because she finds the target's behavioural anomaly intriguing. Because chancing upon him on the street feels providential. Because she wants to know whether the wolf is the next covert link in this chain of fire-walled freelance contractors. For all of these reasons, but especially the last, she doesn't leave. If the wolf does indeed represent the culmination of this job, then for what purpose? As a final witness, to document the target's rictus smile? As a goad, to taunt the dying man? She doesn't need to know, but she wants to know.

*

The wolf can smell the labdanum on the target's clothes as he removes his worn jacket and takes one of the two threadbare armchairs by the cold fireplace. The sweet amber musk of the cathedral. A transfiguration of sorts, from ill-clad old man to priest.

"Tea, Father?"

"No, I've just had a cup, thank you."

A slow smile creeps across the wolf's mouth as he takes the second seat. The priest looks around the sparse interior his pronounced eyes blinking at the mishmash of styles, as if the decorations had been bought wholesale from a bric-a-brac shop.

"It is different from what I expected."

"You mean…? Oh no, this isn't mine. We just rented it for the day. Cash, no questions."

"I don't understand. We?"

The wolf notices his guest running a finger around his collar.

"Perhaps I should open a window, if you are hot?"

"No, just the brisk walk, that's all. My age."

He opens his hands in a gesture of resignation. Big muscular hands, at odds with their moisturised and manicured finishing, no doubt for the benefit of the parishioners, conscientiously maintained as a physical act of respect for the sacraments they are required to handle.

The wolf carefully removes a small, lacquered box from his blazer pocket and balances it on the arm of his chair. His green eyes glitter as he unpacks a small syringe and vial of clear liquid and places these too by his side.

"You are diabetic?"

"Again, no."

"So, what is that?"

"An antidote."

"Whatever for?"

"For you, Father."

The priest uses his handkerchief to wipe away his look of confusion, along with his sweat. "So, you said it was urgent?"

"Oh, it is." The wolf checks his watch. "Before you lose the ability to speak."

Only now does the priest notice the degree to which he is perspiring. He looks to the wolf for an explanation, but receives only a pointedly cool, green stare.

"My child… what have you done?"

*

She shivers from the cold as she speaks quietly

into her mobile, straining to avoid the temptation to shout.

"Yes, well my meeting will overrun, if you could just hold onto her for…?"

She swears silently to the sky as she listens, while also trying to keep her focus on the building across the street.

"Yes, no, I do understand. Overtime… of course."

Distracted by the call, she doesn't see him at first: the wolf, now standing at the first-floor window. Hurriedly, she turns away, using her arm holding the mobile to cover her face and avoid eye contact. Too sudden a move? She feels the sweep of his eyes behind her as he checks up and down the street. Has he noticed her? She cannot be sure.

"Yes, okay, whatever, agreed, I'll be there by then, I've got to go."

She rings off, but keeps entirely still, with her back to the window and the phone still held up at chest height. She taps open the phone's camera function and switches it to selfie mode. Holding her breath, she slowly eases the phone up like a vanity mirror to peer over her shoulder and sneak a glance back at the window. First, her tense face filling the screen. Her frown lines, accentuated. Then, over her shoulder. The window, now with its curtains drawn.

A heavy exhalation. What the hell is she doing? Her only priority should have been her exfiltration. Why risk compromise? Her own voice comes as something of a surprise to her. "Get out of here." But she doesn't. Despite herself, she continues to watch and wait.

*

The interior is now shrouded in an iron-grey diffused gloom from the dusty curtains. The priest writhes on the floor at the wolf's feet, scratching at his own neck as he struggles for breath. He holds up a desperate, outstretched hand for help, for the syringe, but the wolf kicks him back.

"No, no! Not yet. You haven't answered my question."

"I can't. Won't."

The wolf presents his palms in mimicry of the priest's earlier gesture of resignation. Thinner hands, sinewy, with a brutal functionality to the blunt clipping of the nails.

"No name, no antidote."

The priest tries to rally, resolutely staring into the green eyes, refusing to bend.

"Who are you? Why this?"

"We are…" but he checks himself. "We don't have time. More specifically, you don't. Tell me the name. Who did he say?"

The priest shakes his head violently, as much in a desperate attempt to clear a new path for air as in anger.

"No! The Seal of Confession."

The wolf looks down at the wretch with genuine interest. The degree to which the old man is willing to suffer before breaking. The spasms of muscular constriction. The pinpoint pupils. The clawing at the threadbare carpet.

"You can stop this now. His breath for yours."

The wolf reaches for the syringe and delicately decants the clear liquid from the vial. He kneels down by his prey, preparing to administering the life-saving tonic. The promise of salvation.

"One name."

The priest bites at the air, snapping at the shamelessness of the world, of this room, of this man, before finally relenting. He uses the last of his strength to speak, as a low exhale, "Alright…"

The wolf readies the needle.

"Liepins."

The wolf's fern eyes soften, as do his features, in direct opposition to the priest's contortions. Two lives meeting momentarily but heading in opposite directions. Entropy.

"Liepins. Good."

The priest's arm falls forward on the floor, in a desperate invitation to be injected.

"Please."

"Oh, this?"

The wolf rises slowly, calmly, to his feet.

"Sorry, there's no antidote for collaborators like you."

The wolf shrugs his apologies as the priest's twisted face registers the horror of the betrayal.

"But telling me should be your relief. Your confession. Isn't that right?"

The wolf packs away the syringe and vial, barely noticing as the old man convulses for the last time at his feet.

"This is all about doing the right thing, Father. You do see that, don't you? Your pain, for peace. It feels so good to do right, doesn't it? Now, let me see how happy you are, Father. Father?"

The wolf re-pockets the lacquered box, then kicks the old man over onto his back, to reveal his broad cold grimace.

"That's the spirit."

He reaches for his phone.

*

She watches as the door opens and the wolf exits alone. Given the time that has elapsed since the target consumed his tea in the café, it could not be otherwise. That the wolf hasn't called an ambulance, combined with his matter-of-fact manner, confirm that he is the final baton change. From the writer of the pattern-of-life dossier, to her, and now to the wolf: this is a well-organised and well-funded operation. This client is worth sticking with for future business.

The wolf heads by foot in the opposite direction from the station. His gait is light and swift, interrupted only by regular, and expertly conducted, countersurveillance drills: further confirmation, if it were needed, of his status as a professional operator. But as what? She tells herself that she needs to know this information for commercial reasons to understand his service offering, which is evidently distinct enough from her own to require his engagement. To know would enable her to extend her own professional repertoire. She could take a more lucrative slice of any future contract: a new value-adding offering to increase her desirability on the open market. Wetwork is a competitive industry at the best of times; any edge is worth knowing and taking. At least, this is what she tells herself as she walks, following the wolf at a respectful distance.

*

It is over twenty minutes before he turns off the main road, down a side-street, signposted for London Bridge train station. A sensible choice. From here, he will be able to access all of the capital and, even at its quietest, it is a suitably busy terminus to be lost within the crowd. She increases her own bright blue stride to avoid losing him, but then slows as she sees him pass the entrance to the overground trains. She ducks behind the timetable at a nearby bus stop, as she continues to watch him from a distance. His destination must, in fact, be the underground station. But again, to her surprise, he doesn't take the stairs. Instead, he pauses to rummage around in his pocket as he passes one of the area's sleek skyscrapers and then, brandishing a plastic card attached to a brightly coloured lanyard, nods to the building's exterior security guard and heads inside. Astonished, she looks up to see that this is the headquarters of one of the country's main media empires. What on earth is he doing here? There are no through-routes available to him, surely? She edges further up the street and is just able to catch a glimpse of him, through the large ground-floor windows, as he strides through the atrium, ignoring the reception desk entirely, and onto the electronic turnstiles. Sure enough, his plastic card activates the gates. Glass panels slide open in front of him, and he is soon lost in a throng of other employees as they wait for one of the lifts to take them up into the heart of the building. He works there. He is staff.

Chapter Three

The Temple is silent, aside from the far-distant sound of geese hissing their early morning disagreements. Clemency throws a small coin into the margin of the cold dark water: an act of tradition and superstition, an act of devotion to a fickle spirit. She watches her reflection shatter within the peach dawn but can discern nothing beneath the surface. Ancient forms will be stirring in the depths. Gliding shadow-shapes, circling in contemplation of whether to reveal themselves or to remain as obstinate rumours until another day. She is at their behest.

She rests her walking stick on the wet grass and takes her seat. She glances at her watch: a rose-gold Nordgreen, chosen for its Danish simplicity, as well as the manufacturer's commitment to the environment. Inviting an irresponsible brand into such a rarefied space would be verging on the sacrilegious. 06:18. She scans her senses for the slightest movement in her periphery vision, for a degree of temperature change on her cold hands. Nothing.

"It's an enigmatic place, that's for sure," Old John had told her when she'd first been invited to fish this sacred lake. He wasn't exaggerating. The mist lifts from the water reluctantly, as if resentfully having to reveal its definition beneath. This isn't a place that wants to be known.

Her attention turns within. She can feel the incomplete healing deep inside her. Both her shoulder and her thigh, despite the best efforts of the very best surgeons in a discreet London clinic. The unresolved damage done a year before; at the hands of an electric drill in the hands of a Reaper.

"Ten years younger and things may have been different," the trauma specialist had sighed. "But your age…"

He hadn't meant it as an insult, and she hadn't taken it as one, just as a statement of fact. She could see the latent muscular degeneration for herself: physical fault lines etched in shades of white across the x-ray, contour lines mapping her decline in unflinching detail. New damage to an already ageing body. That was the truth of it… is the truth of it. No doctor's bedside manner could disguise the reality. She would heal, but only up to a point.

Despite her best efforts, this realisation caused an inevitable lack of body-confidence that manifested itself gradually, in myriad subtle ways. Initially, it was her tread that changed; each step now more tentative to find a sure footing. Then, she caught herself choosing clothes for their lack of complication rather than their cut. More recently, she has grown out her fringe, to form more of a natural barrier. All these acts initially unconscious, but noticeable over time. Her interior weakness forming as external manifestations, like ugly growths indicating that all is not well with the host body.

It was this evident deterioration that prompted Old John to initiate her into The Temple's enshrouded fellowship a secret he had previously kept from her, despite their many years of friendship. Tucked away from the day-ticket anglers with their loud kit and camaraderie, this private lake is restricted to a select group of anglers, on an invitation-only basis, at Old John's sole discretion and according to an oblique set of criteria of his own making.

"Well, if you're going to make such a meal of it, you should at least catch a clunker," he'd sighed after having watched her struggle on the bank with her stick and injuries, "to make it worth the pain."

She still feels a twinge of humiliation that it took her complete debasement to initiate the invitation, but she is also grateful for his kindness. He was right to appraise that The Temple would be a remedy against her continuing downward spiral. A place where she could replace her all-encompassing sense of inadequacy with a similarly engrossing challenge.

"C'mon." With a wry smile and a beckoning finger, he led her towards a weathered gate at the back of the fishery. Along a small path, through a lush reedy portal and into a parallel world that exists by different rules, as an intersection between the physical and metaphysical, where notions of cause and effect do not tally; where just rewards are not expected; where anything less than total dedication and self-discipline will result in failure. It was the perfect prescription. That of a friend, not a doctor.

The fish within The Temple Lake are scarce, but also magnificent in size and colouration. This is a place of whispered characters. Every one of the specimens is named according to their physical characteristics. The length of their tail. The shape of their eyes. The particular patterning of their scales. They range in age from twenty to fifty years and are as solitary as the few anglers prepared to suffer the inevitable humiliations and discomfits required for their capture. The Temple is for those for whom the struggle is a reward in itself: a sustenance in its own right, until the day The Temple determines to bless them with one of its rare moments of euphoria, if it ever does.

"Can't promise you'll be lucky. But if you are, then you are."

To date, she has not been lucky despite repeated visits, at all times of day and night, and during all the seasons; despite enduring a new level of privation, forgoing all home comforts save for a single chair and flask of hot soup, despite conscientiously pushing aside her own self-pity and self-loathing in accordance with The Temple's demands.

However, the lack of a catch has not blunted her intent. Far from it. She can feel it sharpening her. Because to pay the lake with her time as well as her coins is a necessary part of her devotion and ultimate salvation. An asceticism for deliverance. Like a Shaheed martyr washing as purification before an attack, this is preparation as a manifestation in itself.

The Temple has become her refuge and her place to rebuild. Rising back up the same small incremental steps that evinced her decline. Just as Old John intended. Just as he has provided to others. A curative ladder.

And so, she sits, and she waits, succumbing to The Temple's natural rhythms, however opaque and protracted they may be. Entirely in the moment. Reflected by the water's surface. A mirror to see herself and measure her own progress. With no expectation of catching one of the venue's legends. Because they will not come to her until she is ready.

Chapter Four

She enters the council estate and heads for 'Block D' in accordance with her couriered instructions. The aggressive architectural style was doubtless progressive at the time of its construction. Now, the brutal concrete angles serve only to puncture any dreams of betterment among the residents. She passes the disappointment of single mothers smoking by the paint-worn metal playground and finds the lift. She enters alone and immediately presses the button to close the doors behind her, to ensure that she remains so. There is a silent pause before the jolting surge heralds her ascent.

She watches the first floor pass by, as a sliver of descending light in the small gap between the ill-fitting doors, then she presses the emergency button. No alarms, just a flicker of the lights as the back-up generator is initiated, exactly as anticipated by the supplied paperwork.

She removes a small multitool from her pocket, prises out the screwdriver and sets about removing the metal panel that covers the lift's controls. Sure enough, a foil-wrapped package is tucked among the forest of brightly coloured electrical wires. Holding the panel with one hand, she removes the package with the other, pockets it, then sets about replacing and re-securing the wall section. Only once the interior is as she found it does she tear away a corner of the foil to reveal the heft of used bank notes. Satisfied, she folds away the multitool and restarts the lift on its short journey up to the second floor.

The doors open with a staccato judder and she makes to step out of her metallic confinement. But she stops in her tracks. A pair of lucent green eyes stare back at her. The wolf. She hesitates. To overtly recognise him would be to betray herself, but why would he also be here? To retrieve his own payment? She makes a snap decision in favour of discretion and tries to step to the side of him, but he counters by blocking her path. This is no coincidence.

"Can I help you?"

"You collected the package, yes?"

A surge of relief. He is here for the same reason.

"Yes. But how did you…? When you drew the curtains?"

He bows, fractionally. The lift doors start to close of their own accord. She jams her foot between them to keep them open. The wolf narrows his eyes at her bright-blue shoes.

"A distinctive colour."

She curses herself silently.

"I saw you. And you saw me." There is an understandable chill in his voice. It was entirely unprofessional of her to have followed him. She would feel equally rattled if the tables were turned.

"I was curious, that's all." He shrugs as her prompt to continue. "About your remit. That's all."

"Let me guess, to expand your business offering?"

Caught red-handed, she gives a genuine smile, coupled with a slow sigh. "You got me. I apologise."

He nods his acceptance, all the while keeping a green eye on her hand, which has remained close to her belt buckle. Again, the door starts to close, again she stops it.

"Well, can I ask?"

He can't hide his slight exasperation. "So you can undercut me?"

"Wouldn't you be curious?"

Finally, he yields and gives her a long-overdue smile. She relaxes in kind.

"Pushy, if I may say so."

"Comes with the job. Well?"

"Okay, I'll tell you this, seeing as you've been so persistent…"

She widens her eyes in anticipation. He pauses for theatrical effect.

"Curiosity…"

She is fractionally too late. By the time she has finished the rest of the saying in her head, a deep-red circle has already appeared just below her hairline. The suppressed shot was barely audible.

"You know the rest."

The wolf moves quickly to follow the crumpled woman back into the lift as she slides down the far wall, leaving a smear of blood in her wake. He removes the foil packet and the briefing paperwork from her pocket and the concealed weapon from her waistband holster, presses the button to close the lift doors using his jacket to avoid leaving prints, then walks away briskly to the emergency stairs, and down, out of the estate.

Chapter Five

Clemmie struggles to pack away her few pieces of fishing equipment into the back of her car. Old John is leaning against a nearby gate, watching on gleefully.

"I'm not offering to help out of respect, not a lack of manners, you understand."

She resists the desire to swear at him and tries again. "I'm on the mend, thank you." She finally manages to slam down the boot with conspicuous aggression.

"I can see that alright!"

She laughs despite herself, then turns to face him with a milder expression. "No, really, thank you."

"Don't mention it. No luck?"

"I'm beginning to suspect the lake's actually empty. One of your jokes."

"Ah, so you're admitting defeat?"

"That's not what I said."

"Hard to tell…what with all the whining." Old John watches her closely as she tries to suppress a smirk. There is a near-paternal tenderness in his eyes. "It's good to see you laughing again."

"That wasn't a laugh."

"Right."

"And maybe if you were funnier, I'd laugh more?"

"Ha! Very good. Well, quite good, that."

She arranges herself behind the modified steering wheel. A plastic attachment has been fitted so it can be manoeuvred with the use of just one hand.

"Very fancy."

"It's surprisingly easy to use. Even you should manage it."

"And just think of all the things I could do with m'spare hand, eh?"

She starts the engine and turns up the radio to suppress the sound of him laughing at another of his own jokes. It's one of the talk stations: a discussion about the new level of military cooperation between America, Germany and Poland. But, to Old John's evident delight, she has to simultaneously turn off the engine and the radio, while also struggling for the phone which is now vibrating in her pocket. He wanders off, laughing at the sky as she takes the call.

"Hello? Yes. Understood. Text it to me."

*

Old John is still giggling to himself as he serves the next customer from his ramshackle bailiff's hut. He watches Clemmie drive past and gives her a wave. "Don't wave back now, mind… or you'll have to stop the car again!" He can just make out the gesture she gives him with her spare hand before she eases her car out of the fishery. The sound of Old John's renewed laughter echoes down the leafy lane behind her.

Chapter Six

Clemmie approaches the wooden cottage from the seafront pedestrian walkway. The dull rhythm of her walking stick echoes off the stocky stone tidal wall that stretches around the bay. The shingle shelves off below, ordered by heavy wooden groyes, towards the green-grey sea. The smell of vegetal decay blusters around her as she surveys each of the converted fishermen's huts, distinguishable by their designer gardens and idiosyncratic pastel colouring. However, despite each owner's best efforts to impose their own character onto these one hundred and fifty-year-old buildings, the latent architectural personality wins out, trenchantly bridling at the audacity of today's occupants, forcing them to bow down to a more powerful agency that has no truck with their money and London reputations. This is a natural surging energy, provoked by the sea: the essential character of Whitstable.

She finds her destination and knocks at the bright blue paint flecked door, but there is no answer. She takes a seat on the nearby weathered wooden bench, and contemplates the yellow flower heads, the silver foliage and the spicy scent of the curry plants that line the perimeter of the balcony area. She doesn't know when or why the Chief bought this bolthole perhaps as a physical getaway in case of threat, or maybe as a mental sanctuary to purge those mission-memories that can't be flushed out by talking therapies. Then again, maybe he bought it more recently in anticipation of his retirement; it is only a matter of time.

After five minutes, he slowly shuffles his way back through the front gate and smiles his welcome while also doing his best to clench a pipe.

"You look like a proper mariner."

He offers a phlegm-rich cough of appreciation as he waves the smouldering briar in her general direction. "My GP's idea. God love her. All the nicotine, less of the emphysema. So she says." He now holds up a plastic bag by way of an explanation. "Lunch. Worth the wait, I promise."

*

They eat their oysters, shucked by the Chief's old hands, at the rough wooden kitchen table. A mix of shallots and red-wine vinegar as an accompaniment, served with a worn silver teaspoon from a chipped porcelain cup. Clemmie notices the two-tone colouration of the spoon: a clear demarcation line on the spoon's bowl; glistening silver abruptly switching to blue-grey tarnish on the shoulders and along the thread the effect of regular immersion in the acidic vinegar mix and an indication of the Chief's preference for this meal. She feels a renewed sense of intimacy between them, as much for having been invited into his closely guarded personal life as for admission into his hush-hush coastal bolthole.

"These are the Royal natives." He wafts his hand towards the window. "From the flats over there, by the wind farm."

Clemmie examines the small shell with its succulent pearly flesh.

"And the bigger ones here, these are the Rock Oysters. Non-natives. Imposters. Brash. Taste: you'll see."

She downs the two in succession. "Certainly sweeter."

"The Royals? Course they are. More refined."

She smiles at his characteristic superiority. Blue-blooded to a fault.

"So…" He uses his pipe for punctuation. "Priest. Dead. You've read about it?" Clemmie shakes her head as she helps herself to another, royal, oyster. "Good. At least we're still able to muzzle some of the hacks." He pauses to cough before continuing, "Orthodox."

"Greek?"

"Russian."

"And what was the motive, for his murder?"

"Who said it was murder?"

"You called me. Hardly likely to have been

diabetes, is it?"

He grumbles a chuckle as he sucks at the ebonite stem, a faded white dot on its polished top surface. The smoke drifts in her direction, but he offers no apology. It has a distinctive soapy note that she recognises. Aside from the hay-like smell of the Virginias and the earthiness of the Burleys, there is a perfumed topping characteristic of the *Lakeland* style. Just one of the many details she has stored away over the years to help with target recognition.

"We wouldn't be interested normally, only..." He tamps down the tobacco with his finger and sips at the bit to stoke the embers fully into life. "He's important. Was. Well, not him exactly, but his congregation. The great and the good of the Russian community in London. If that's not a contradiction in terms."

"There's one in the House of Lords now. A Russian."

He shakes his head in slow despair. "So they tell me, but my point still stands."

"Yes sir."

"The Russian Ambassador is a regular at the church."

Clemmie, is noticeably more intrigued. "Right."

The Chief reaches back and retrieves a file. He hands over one photo from within: the corpse, on the cheap carpet, between the two threadbare armchairs.

The grimace.

"The priest? He'd upset Mother Russia?"

The Chief breathes smoke from the edges of his clenched teeth, like a paternal dragon. "That was our first, *obvious* thought. But their embassy has launched its own investigation."

"So, if it wasn't them: Russian mafia?"

Another withering look through the blue haze. "And that's assessed based on the last airport novel you've read, is it?"

Clemmie blanches at his scalding tone. He now hands over a second photo: a woman in a lift with a bullet hole in her forehead. "Freelance wet worker known as 'Polly'. A lot prettier before the head wound."

"What's the evidence of a link?"

"Residue of the poison in the gutter outside her flat."

Clemmie nods as she studies the photo more closely. "And the smile?"

"*Oenanthe crocata.* Slow acting. Constricts the muscles. Torture of a kind."

"Certainly sends a message. But to whom?"

"Exactly." Whatever he was up to, or whatever entered his confessional ear was evidently worth knowing. Something someone other than the Russians wants to know. And that makes it valuable.

Something I'd rather like to know first."

"So that's the brief?"

"Get me the facts. Then contain the situation as necessary. We've kept her body off the radar for the time being, which gives you an edge over the Ruskies." He finally hands over the rest of the file, then gets to his feet with a wheeze and starts clearing the table as Clemmie rifles through the various papers. She can't contain her smile as she notices two of the photos. The Chief provides commentary from the sink. "Yes, your old team. I've had them sleeping for the last year. Time to wake them up."

Next, Clemmie pulls out details of a London address.

"Your new home. Nothing fancy. But serviceable." He returns to the table and leans close, his voice more tender. "That's if you want to take on something connected to Russia?"

"And why wouldn't I?"

"I can understand if this…" he gestures to her walking stick, "brought it all back: your previous experience there."

"It's in the past. Really."

"Good. I expected nothing less." He returns the empty oyster shells to their original plastic bag. "Brash imposters."

"The Russians?"

He examines one of the shells. "But they make a surprisingly good mulch when you crush them. Suddenly they become useful. Bring me something actionable."

"Yes sir."

Chapter Seven

Stig is already waiting at the subterranean café within the Vauxhall underground station. He sits facing the staircase that leads down from street level. At first, Clemmie doesn't recognise him. Gone are the long shaggy hair, beard and stooped demeanour. This is an altogether more well-turned-out young man: cropped, trimmed and alert, redolent of a budding accountant rather than the beatnik tenderfoot she had known just a year before. At their last meeting, he had saved her life. The time before that, just a few hours earlier, he had made the decision to leave the service. He had come back to rescue her of his own accord, as a civilian. She would never forget that.

He sees her, and ignores her, long before she completes her countersurveillance drills and slides in alongside him on the café's communal bench. She speaks her greeting into her cup as she takes her first sip. "Hello, stranger."

He gives a slight bow of the head. "You haven't changed. Apart from the stick." They survey the empty staircase in front of them. Stig checks his watch. "In precisely four minutes, the first of the commuters will start coming down. Keep watching."

"For anything particular?"

"Just watch. A personal project I'm doing."

Clemmie does as instructed. "We've been summoned."

"I assumed this wasn't a social call."

"Are you in?"

He sighs heavily, then checks his watch. "Three minutes."

Clemmie looks at him quizzically, then back at the stairs.

"Maybe."

"What's the Chief had you doing all this time?"

"Nothing. Waiting. He said I should take some time to consider my future. No rush. So, this is decision time?"

"Yes, it is."

"Personal projects. What I've been doing to keep myself busy. Two minutes."

"I'm intrigued."

"Moments of beauty. To make up for all the mess, from before."

Clemmie resists the urge to press him. If this is his way of coping, then so be it. Whatever it is, it's likely better than reaching for a bottle. She exhales pointedly across the top of her paper cup, but not to cool its contents. Stig reaches for his mobile phone and prepares the camera. They hear a bus pull up on the street above. The release of compressed air from the opening doors. The sound of footsteps.

"Here we go. Thirty, twenty-nine, eight…"

Right on time, a herd of commuters reaches the top of the staircase and begins its bustling descent: a sea of frustration and jockeying, advancing to the ticket barriers and awaiting trains. A slight smile twitches at the edges of Clemmie's mouth. "Ah, I see. How very… poetic."

In front of them, each individual traveller is becoming an unwitting player in a piece of performance art.

"It's all along the top step. They can't see it because of the angle of approach."

As the commuters step onto the staircase, they tread into one of Stig's hidden pools of brightly coloured paint, which they then distribute down the rest of the stairs behind them, unaware of the kaleidoscope of colour they are leaving in their wake. With each new wave of arrivals, the interior is gradually transformed from its original functional grey, into a spectacular spectrum that spills down into the station with decreasing intensity. Stig uses his phone to document the moment as Clemmie enjoys the show.

"I like it. The concept and the execution."

With the arrival of the confused station staff, Stig

re-pockets his phone and finally turns to face his former boss. "Thank you."

"And can I assume you don't take credit for these…?"

"Inhabited metaphors, that's what I call them."

Again, Clemmie resists the urge to mock. She nods him on.

"One of the benefits of living a covert life. I'm a myth in the art world."

This time her laughter gets the better of her. "Well, *Myth*, if you've finished your masterpiece, and before we get lifted, perhaps we could have a chat?"

Chapter Eight

They walk through the elegant city gardens, nursing their coffees. The last of the morning's commuters head for the nearby underground station. Stig smiles to himself as he watches them pass; en route to becoming unwitting participants in his ongoing guerrilla artwork. Clemmie finally breaks the silence. "Do you think you're over it?"

"It wouldn't be right for me to complain, seeing as what happened to you."

"And I wouldn't be here if it wasn't for you. This shoulder works fine. Use it."

He takes a deep breath. "My issue is with the misguided presumption to save. It's deluded and egotistical. All of it." He smiles at Clemmie's nonplussed look. "You did ask."

"I did."

"I've used the downtime to read, as well as…" He gestures back towards the tube station. "Dostoevsky, *Notes from the Underground*, *Crime and Punishment*, that kind of thing."

"Right. So, you disagree with our work… philosophically?"

"That was the itch I felt before. But I didn't have the words to describe it. Now I do."

Clemmie watches a magpie hop around one of the bins, searching for scraps. "Go on."

"What we're doing is a form of saviour complex. These jobs, these people; they haven't asked for help, but we get stuck in any way, for our own sense of virtue, to be seen to be busy, so the Chancellor increases our budget next year. The entire service is fabricated on a manufactured worth."

Clemmie waves her stick to scare off the bird. "You don't honestly believe that, do you?"

He shrugs, then takes a seat on one of the wooden benches. "Is it another Black Op?"

"Yes."

"And Louise, will you reactive her as well?"

"That's my hope, yes."

"And the job?"

"You know I can't... not unless you're on the bus."

"What happens if I pass?"

"Then I find someone else."

"So, you have others?"

"None like you, Stig, trust me. A myth no less. Or you could get out now, as you said you wanted."

They watch the hopeful squirrels approaching from a distance.

"It was Louise's idea. Coming back for you. If we… You need to know that."

"And why did you agree?"

"It felt right."

"Perhaps that tells you something; whether this work is for you."

"Nah, we just knew you'd mess things up by yourself."

Clemmie laughs abruptly. "Well, on that, you may well have been right. So, any chance you'd save me from making a mess of this job? I'm asking you if that helps? No saviour complex. Give it some philosophical thought."

He nods as she reaches for her stick and makes to get to her feet.

"Hang on, where are you going?"

"To let you think about it."

"Yeah… and I have. I'm in."

She looks at him in open-mouthed wonder. "That's it? After all the soul-searching? The philosophical angst?"

"Well, yeah. I could just do with the money at the moment to be honest."

Clemmie laughs hard enough to scare the squirrels back into their trees. "You're a strange one, you know that, Stig?"

Chapter Nine

The three-bedroomed flat is on Glasford Street, off Mitcham Road, a ten-minute walk from Tooting Broadway underground station: first floor, with its own private entrance and the Chief's assurance that the flats above and below are empty and appropriately secured. From the outside the premises looks like just another tired old, white-rendered, terraced house that has been diced into flats for seasonal students or prostitutes.

Clemmie and Stig take different routes around the building to inspect its every detail before heading, separately, through the characterless door and up the narrow stairwell to the mouldy interior with its scattering of takeaway boxes in every room. With work, it will be serviceable.

They regroup in the small kitchenette as Stig searches for a kettle but finds none. "No expense spared."

"It's bleak. Granted."

"Shall I sort it out a bit?"

"Thank you. Usual kit, and some Russian dictionaries."

Stig widens his eyes expectantly. "Russian?"

"Soon, let's just wait 'til we're all together."

Clemmie settles herself at the seventies laminated table – one of the few items of furniture in the entire premises – and hooks her stick onto the back of the plastic chair. There is a knock at the door, and Stig heads out. A few moments later, Louise enters the kitchen and lights up the room with her smile. She races around the table and crumples around her former boss.

"Am I glad to see you! Oh sorry, sorry."

"No, it's fine."

"No, I'm sorry, does it still hurt?"

"It's fine."

They examine each other enthusiastically, before being enveloped by a gradual awkward silence.

"So, here we are."

"Again."

"Like…before."

Clemmie looks Louise over. Her thick black hair is longer now, tied back in a single plait. She also looks more toned, as if she has spent a considerable amount of the past year committed to training. "You look in great shape."

"A year of cyber-training, it was either get fat or get fit. And you?"

"Good."

"Good."

The silence forces itself between them again until Stig finally steps forward to take charge. "So what did we do last time? When we first met?"

"We went for a drink."

"Well?"

Nods all round.

*

They nurture their beers, still in silence. The pub is a typical Tooting affair; rough at the edges with an assortment of loners sitting at individual tables reading the *Racing Post* and keeping an eye on the televised early afternoon meetings. Even when these wiry social islands do go to the bar to reorder, they seem determined to sustain their isolation, avoiding conversation with each other and the bar staff. Like a shoal of tragic fish, they congregate by type but keep their constant distance.

Louise makes a point of lowering her voice to a whisper:

"Is this…a call-up?"

"If you would like. There is a job."

Louise discreetly pumps her fist with delight at the news.

"Can I take that as a yes?"

"Instead of more geek classes? Too right you can!" Now, turning to Stig: "You've already agreed?"

"The same reaction as you. Identical."

Clemmie swallows her smile, then it's back to silence. Finally, she leans in: "Right. Well, if we're done with the social chit-chat?" She produces two file copies from her bag and discreetly slides them across the table.

"Priest: Russian. Wet worker: British. She killed him. We don't know why, or who killed her."

"Let me guess, he's a dissident or connected to the mafia?"

"You get that from the last airport novel you read?" Stig looks wounded but Clemmie gives him a reassuring smile. "My first reaction too, if it makes you feel better?" He seems placated. "Have them read by this evening. See what you can assess. I'll meet you back at the flat at eighteen hundred. I'm assuming whatever personal life you may have can be rescheduled for a few weeks? Good, because we have a meet tonight."

The others give her an expectant look. "You gonna say who?"

"Vespers."

Chapter Ten

The cathedral is tucked away at the end of a small cul-de-sac within London's South Kensington. It can be smelt before it can be seen. Tentacles of sweet incense reach through the imposing double wooden doors, encircle the small exterior square and then ease their way down the neighbouring streets, feeling for the desperate and the devout. The fragrance is particular – an unctuous blend from a faraway land – and entirely incongruous with the surrounding architecture. An otherness on the wind.

Stig peels off just before the entrance and takes a position in one of the square's ill-lit corners. Clemmie and Louise draw shawls over their heads and make their way through the porch and into the busy nave. On entering, the first impression is one of enchanted opulence. Incense and monophonic chanting swirl around the forest of silhouetted figures as they stand, facing the gleaming altar doors. The building's walls are adorned with icons of all shapes and scenes. Their frames and gold-leaf backgrounds glitter in the light from the many candle-stands. Each painting is a glimpse into a tumultuous world of stylised angels and demons, although every saint maintains the same expression of serene Byzantine indifference.

The two women position themselves within the shadows at the back of the left-hand aisle and survey the ritualised behaviour all around them. Rather than the formal seated congregation of a Church of England service, these Orthodox worshippers are here as participants, not observers. Each new person who enters, crosses themselves three times before kneeling to touch their forehead to the cool marble floor. After this, they make their way back to a rudimentary wooden kiosk by the entrance doors and buy thin beeswax candles from a forthright old woman, wearing a head scarf as pale blue as her near-transparent eyes. They then jostle their way through the crowd and install their prayer candles in one of the already-bristling towers of fire dotted throughout the cavernous interior. Next, each worshipper hunts down their preferred icon from the many available options – presumably in accordance with the saint or angel's professed metaphysical powers – and kisses the frame or the glass, behind which the painted board is ensconced. Finally, with their spiritual preparations complete, the worshipper takes their place on either side of the church according to their gender; women and children along one aisle, and men grouped along the other.

On account of her stick, Clemmie is provided with a wooden chair by a young woman who is busy collecting spent candles, presumably to recycle their wax. Moments later, a richly decorated priest emerges from the sanctuary through an ornate altarpiece door, and the service is ready to begin in earnest. From a hidden balcony above, the chanting voices – male and female – change their tempo. The previous lyricism is replaced by more discernible biblical verses, first in Russian, then in English. Staccato stanzas, repetition upon repetition, an incantation that fills the entire cathedral with a new transfigurative energy a resonance that reshapes the congregation into a cohesive whole of whispered worship.

Unlike other denominations, the priest faces the altar doors – the iconostasis – throughout the service, with his back to his flock. The message is clear: this rotund man in his early sixties is in no way superior, despite his elaborate garb. The entire cathedral of followers is unified by humility: hoping and praying for a sign, an intervention or some temporary solace.

After forty minutes of standing, kneeling and collective murmuring, the service nears its end. A younger priest helps his companion to light yet more incense within a censer, which the senior man then swings ahead of him as he encircles the interior space, urging the collective prayers to mix with the fragrant smoke and rise higher, towards an invisible ear.

*

Clemmie and Louise keep a prudent distance as

they wait for the priest to share a few private words with each member of the congregation as they depart. He pays as much earnest attention to the svelte, fox-clad women, who all seem to share a plastic surgeon, as to the quivering poor. It is a further thirty minutes of his whispered advice, consolations and blessings before he registers the two remaining women and approaches them with benign intrigue.

"Ladies. You are visiting us together? I don't think I recognise you?"

Clemmie offers her hand but he ignores it, preferring to keep his latticework of fingers resting on his sizeable midriff.

"We're not here for devout reasons, I'm afraid."

"Ты из посольства?"

"We also don't know Russian."

"I asked if you are also from the Embassy - evidently not."

"Ah, they have been already?"

"Perhaps you are the British police, yes?"

Clemmie notices the younger priest trying to listen inconspicuously from his place at one of the brass candle-stands. "Actually, is there somewhere else we could talk?"

The old priest thinks, then calmly nods. "My name is Father Gregory."

"It's a pleasure to meet you, Father."

"And you...?"

Clemmie dodges the question, clumsily, with a smile. "We... are waiting for you to show us where we can talk."

He accepts her sleight with a subservient bow. "Well, come this way please," he says leading them to an adjoining corridor.

*

Stig watches as the last of the congregation leaves the cathedral. Moments later, the young priest appears to see them on their way and, to lock up. Despite Stig's best efforts to remain hidden, he is visible within the darkness.

"Hello?" The priest can just make out a moment of hesitation from the shadows. "Are you okay, my son?"

Stig finally steps into the light with an embarrassed smile. "Perhaps a little too old to be your son?"

"A figure of speech, of course. My name is Father Lev. Can I help you? Are you in trouble?"

"God, no. I mean, no, thank you. Just waiting for my friends. They came to the service."

"The two women? The police?"

He sees Stig's slight exasperation, so drops his voice. "Ah, I see. And that is why you are also hiding in the dark, yes?"

Stig tries to laugh it off, quietly.

"Perhaps I can offer you some tea while you wait then? I'm sorry, I didn't catch your name?"

"Bryan. Yes, tea would be great, thank you."

*

Father Gregory shows the two women into a spacious room that is clearly used for Bible study groups. On two sides, the walls are covered with floor-to-ceiling bookcases with multiple copies of the same study texts. Against the far wall, there is a trestle table with an electric Russian samovar that steams away quietly, sending occasional drifts of vapour through the forest of nearby stacked plastic chairs. The priest sets about removing several of the chairs before Louise steps in to help him.

"Thank you."

They take their seats in a tight circle at the centre of the room. Father Gregory interlinks his fingers across his belly once again in patient expectation. Clemmie speaks slowly, choosing her words with evident care. "I'd like to offer my, our, sincere condolences for your recent loss."

"Father Igor rests with God now. That is a blessing, not a matter for remorse. Despite the nature of the tragedy."

"Of course. Still, I'm sure he was a close friend of yours." The old priest nods, almost knowingly. Clemmie notices a slight aloofness in his manner, but continues nonetheless. "And I'm sure you'll want to help us find out who could have committed this atrocity, and why?" To Clemmie's consternation, Father Gregory shakes his head and looks to the heavens, smiling. "I'm sorry, is there something I said?" she adds.

"The surprise, my child, is on account of you using the exact same question tree as my compatriots from the Embassy. *'For the sake of your friend.'*" Clemmie slowly raises her hands in surrender. He leans in and examines his guests with slow, deliberate eyes. "Perhaps people in your line of work share a rather unflattering opinion of people in my line of work?" He brandishes the large golden cross on the heavy chain around his neck. "Because we wear these, we are somehow gullible? I would just mention that we also studied question trees in seminary school."

Louise snorts a laugh at the extent to which Clemmie has been owned by the old man. She tries to clear the air: "Can I suggest that we start this again?"

Clemmie and Father Gregory share a respectful smile and nod of agreement. The priest is the first to speak. "Good. And, with that in mind, honesty would of course be appropriate given our location. You chose, rather clumsily if I may say so, to avoid telling me your names?" This time it is Clemmie who laughs, in exasperation. Another direct hit. Clemmie is in no doubt she has met her match. Despite his portly deportment, Father Gregory is as wily as he is disarming. He is perhaps the perfect priest to deal with the egos, vanities and self-aggrandisements of the Russian community in this premium area of London. His flock don't stand a chance. Clemmie watches him with due deference as he, in turn, watches Louise looking to her boss for guidance. A silent standoff. "I would remind you that God sees the truth in everything."

Clemmie finally gives a nod.

"Louise."

"Clemency."

"Well, the pleasure is mine. And now that our way is the truth, where shall we start?"

*

Stig follows Father Lev to the end of the corridor and into a small dining hall. As in the cathedral itself, the room's walls are decorated with a multitude of icons.

"You will have it the Russian way, with lemon?"

"Okay. Sure." Stig is drawn to the images that surround him on all sides. He steps closer to examine several of the pieces. "They're beautiful."

The priest joins him, teas in hand. "Not to my eyes."

"How so? Just look at them."

"Functional, awe-inspiring, but not beautiful." Stig looks again, as if from the other's perspective. "You know how they're painted? In a state of prayer. Each one is a window. A direct, living, connection with the subject."

"Like they're alive?"

"In a manner of speaking."

"Inhabited metaphors. I love that." The priest can see that Stig is genuinely engrossed. Together, they examine a depiction of a male figure dressed in a crimson cloak, with golden wings blossoming from his shoulders. In his hands he carries a sword and a small globe. "And him? Is he an angel?"

"'Is', that is good: the present tense. Not 'was'. I think you understand us?" Father Lev gestures for them to sit at one of the tables. "An archangel. Michael. '*As captain of the army of the Lord, I am now come.*' That's from Joshua."

"And what does that mean? That he's there when you need to kick arse?"

Father Lev tries to stifle his inappropriate laugh at the inappropriate joke. "I could never endorse such a thing, obviously."

"Obviously."

"It's interesting though that he reached out to you; don't you think?" Stig is about to interject but then stops, intrigued. "Oh, you believe that you chose to look at him, not the other way around? As you wish. But perhaps he is relevant? For your line of work?"

Stig smiles at the idea, but the young priest doesn't. "I don't think angels, archangels even, would want to get involved in my line of work."

"But you do fight on the side of right, don't you?"

Another smile from Stig, but this one is thinner than the first. "Now that's a very good question."

"Essential, I would have thought, Bryan?"

*

Clemmie and Louise wait respectfully as Father Gregory composes his thoughts.

"There are occasions when the underworld appears to us, and we see it as if for the first time. The degree of its malevolence. Father Igor's passing was one of those occasions."

"And as to a possible motive?"

"That is for God alone to know."

Clemmie rolls her eyes. "With respect, we work in rather more rational terms."

Again, he takes the necessary time to pick his words. "Our calling requires us to hear things that, by their very existence, their sheer wickedness, remind us exactly of God's grace."

"You mean in confession?"

"I do not remember saying that so crudely."

Clemmie smiles away the slight. "Please, continue."

"If, hypothetically, Father Igor had heard

something, and if, theoretically, it had influenced his behaviour, skewed his own affiliations even, well, as his spiritual father and confessor, the Seal of Confession would forbid me from revealing it. Even if to do so would help you 'rationally', as you would have it."

"This is to solve a murder. It takes precedence."

"Over God?"

"In terms of the law."

Louise leans across to seize the priest's focus away from Clemmie. "What I think we mean, Father, is that we respect your faith, and its customs, entirely. However, were such a situation to ever take place, what changes in behaviour might you see… have seen?"

Clemmie gives Louise an ironic smile of thanks for the intervention. "What she said."

The priest speaks to Louise. "Well, the individual priest may exhibit the sort of isolation characteristics that would be indicative of emerging extremist sympathies. Increased anger and an inability to discuss all views on certain subjects."

Both women double-take. Louise gives Clemmie a 'told you so' look. "Those are very particular descriptions, Father. Textbook signs of radicalisation. The seminary?"

"We are at the frontline just as much as you. Our counter-radicalisation training reflects that."

The atmosphere in the room shifts. A new respect

has been established between Louise and the priest. "And sadly, we have form. The Russian Orthodox Church, I mean." Louise gestures for him to continue. "The sixteenth century. You had the dissolution of the monasteries; we had a similar tension between Church and state. Between the possessors and the non-possessors. A Church of land and wealth, worldly power even, or a humbler manifestation of God's will, as the soul and conscience of the nation."

Louise gestures around her. "It doesn't take an ecclesiastical scholar to see that the *haves* won that particular argument." Father Gregory chooses not to comment. Louise sighs as she repositions herself in her chair. "Okay, so let's just say this historical tension still existed, today, hypothetically." He nods, fractionally. "With Church and state so close, that would make being a *have not* a rather serious issue, wouldn't it?"

"A modern non-possessor. Given our Patriarch's political friendships, yes."

"In fact, that would make such a person a *dissident* in some people's eyes. Those political friends, for example. However honourable the individual's religious convictions."

Father Gregory winces: "In that instance, the line between Church and state could indeed become a fault line."

Louise studies him. His face remains pained, as if

recollecting. "What is it? There is something else, Father?"

He looks up, as if speaking to another audience. "That would be enough to bear. To contain even. But then…"

"Yes, Father?"

His voice is laden with tired disappointment. "Hidden hands. Exploiting. For their worldly masters. Undermining His house for their own agendas." Suddenly his eyes flash with fury as he refocuses on the two women. "Who do they think they are?!"

Both women widen their eyes at this. Clemmie now re-joins the conversation. "You tell me." Father Gregory regains his composure, sits upright, almost to attention, then shakes his head apologetically but resolutely.

"Oh, let me guess, the bloody Seal of Confession?!"

Louise leans across Clemmie for a second time, to calm things: "I wonder, Father, did you have a similarly hypothetical conversation with your own embassy staff? You said they visited?"

He shakes his head solemnly. "Alas, they weren't even prepared to tell me their real names. And without truth how can there be illumination? *'I am the way, and the truth, and the life. No one comes to the Father except through me.'*"

Louise makes sure to maintain eye contact as she

nods her understanding. "But why not be honest? Unless they are intending to use the situation for their own political ends?"

He is more desperate again now. "Why indeed? Here of all places. The house of God?!"

Louise reaches across and places her hand on his. "We will do what we can. Discreetly. To find answers and make this go away. How's that?"

He studies her before speaking. "So young, and with such living grace. Wouldn't you say, Clemency?"

"Oh, I tell her constantly."

He flicks his eyes between the two women as if comparing their particular styles. "And you don't believe in the power of grace?" It is said as a statement, despite being a question.

Clemmie has had enough, she repositions herself in her chair. "I'll tell you what I know for a fact, vicar! If we leave this room without something to go on, you'll need more than grace to save your church here in London. Am I making myself clear?"

Louise blanches at Clemmie's takeover. Father Gregory gets to his feet and straightens his cross with a sigh. "It's a cathedral. And I will of course pray for you both." He turns first to Louise, "For your divine favour," then hands Clemmie her stick, "and for your continued recovery."

Clemmie stands to face him. "I'll put my faith in

medicine, if it's all the same to you. Facts."

He winces at the crude brutality of her approach, then rocks back and forth on the spot, as if weighing up his options. "Then perhaps I could suggest somewhere that delivers results for someone of your rational persuasion?"

"A clinic?"

"A country."

She crosses her arms, level with the cross on his chest, as if waiting for him to prove himself to her. "Go on."

"I've heard it whispered that Latvia has everything for the rationalist seeking remedies."

Clemmie seems pleased with his ultimate acquiescence. "Good. We will look into that. Thank you."

He manufactures a conciliatory smile. "Think of it as a divine intervention."

Chapter Eleven

Clemmie and Louise pore over their laptops. Clemmie passes Louise a pamphlet: the cathedral's timetable. "It says Divine Liturgy starts at nine on a Sunday."

Louise snatches the paper and resumes tapping into her computer. "Was there a need to be quite so rude?"

"He was stalling. Couldn't you tell? Confession takes place from eight, you seen that?"

Louise nods. "Yup. But I had him. He would've given me the same information."

"If you say so." She hands over another document. "And here are the dates Father Igor was in the hot seat."

"I do say so!" Clemmie realises that Louise is genuinely offended. She sets aside her papers to show that she is taking this seriously. Louise continues, quietly, "We just have different styles, Clem, that's all."

Clemmie sighs slow and long. "You're right." She gestures to the documents. "You would have got this anyway, whereas I just got frustrated."

"Not better or worse, just different. And my style

works too."

"Right. One hundred percent. I'm sorry." Louise nods that the apology has been accepted and they get back to work. Clemmie speaks with more care now. "If you could just check from an hour before…"

Distracted, Louise interrupts. "I know, Oyster cards, taxi fares, parking apps. However they travelled there, they'll have left a trace."

"Exactly." Clemmie sits back and watches the younger woman. Her studiousness. Her quiet assurance. Her dexterity at the keyboard. Perfectly in control of herself and her work. Her smile is both proud and pained, as if watching her younger self.

Louise feels the intensity of her stare. "What?"

"You know, he was right."

"Who?"

"You are great at this."

Suddenly embarrassed, Louise stops her tapping. "Alright, don't overdo it. I only said we have different styles."

"No, seriously. You are. It's good to be working with you again."

Louise narrows her eyes suspiciously, unsure if Clemmie is being sincere. She is. "Thank you. That means a lot. Now, that's enough."

They resume their individual tasks, now with a slight awkwardness between them. The silence becomes deafening, until finally punctured by giggling from behind Clemmie's laptop screen.

"What now?"

"'Living grace.'"

"Oh, piss off."

"Now that wasn't very graceful!"

To their evident relief, Stig enters with the first of the items to redecorate the flat. "We have coffee, hurrah! Anyone?"

"I'll make it."

"No, let me."

Both women get up and race for the kitchen to break the tension. They laugh as they pass. "Stig, have I told you recently how brilliant you are, by the way?"

"What?"

"Seriously, a myth among men."

"Eh?"

Utterly confused, Stig remains standing with his toilet brush, bin bags and other assorted groceries.

Chapter Twelve

Stig proudly surveys his handiwork. The flat has been transformed into a serviceable, if basic, operations centre. The standard setup: a central table in the main room with designated seating areas, the start of a storyboard on one of the walls within the small bedroom and frosted paper over the most conspicuous windows as a matter of habit rather than need. The diffused light gives the interior an aethereal quality: a parallel world with its own particular rules.

"Four names." Louise repositions her laptop on the table for the others to see. "Although, we can likely discount two. They have the same surname, *Krumins*, and arrive by car."

Clemmie closes her own laptop to give Louise her full attention. "So how do you know there's two of them?"

"One parking payment, but a debit card in the same name regularly buys two ice creams just after the service, from this café here. A parent and child."

"Okay. And the others?"

"Two Latvian surnames. Both arrive by bus, but apart. *Liepins* and *Andersons*."

"And no other payments in the area that could give us more clues?"

Louise shakes her head. Clemmie turns to Stig. "So, there's your brief." He replies with a quizzical look. "The younger priest. Can you develop him?"

"Father Lev. Sure. He's cool. We discussed art."

"Maybe he'd be keen to see your masterpieces? Find out what he knows."

"On it." With evident relish, he hands over a toilet brush and bleach to Louise, "All yours, thanks," then heads to his own desk area and writes the two names of interest into his phone.

Swearing under her breath, Louise reluctantly trudges off to clean the toilet, but Clemmie waves her back. "That can wait. We're all headed in the same direction. And Louise, bring your passport."

With comparable satisfaction, Louise places the cleaning products back on Stig's desk in front of him. "In case you get back before us."

Chapter Thirteen

The taxi pulls over and Clemmie and Louise alight, but Stig stays put. Clemmie leans through the open window. "Head back to the flat afterwards."

Over her shoulder, Stig sees Louise miming cleaning a toilet but chooses not to take the bait. "Right."

The taxi pulls away, with Stig directing the driver to the cathedral, just a few side streets farther along the main road. Clemmie and Louise turn to face the imposing metal gates that lead to the private enclave in which the Russian Embassy is situated. The fact that this is one of the most expensive residential streets on the planet is self-evident. Known locally as *Billionaires' Row*, Kensington Palace Gardens is permanently guarded by a mix of fearsome private security and Diplomatic Protection Group officers on account of the multiple embassies, oligarchs and members of international royalty who have chosen this location for their ostentatious London residences.

There is no access without a confirmatory call from the sentry. The two women state they are here to discuss Father Igor. Sure enough, within just a few minutes, the Russian Embassy has called back granting their admission. They make their way past an array of perimeter security, including dogs and cameras, until they reach the metal revolving gate that grants access to 5-7, the Russian Embassy. A small, tight-faced man is already waiting for them on the other side of the fence. The curl of transparent plastic behind his ear, coupled with the bulge of a discreet weapon under his blazer, indicates he is part of the security detail.

"I have been told to escort you inside. Please."

He presses a button. The heavy turnstile is released. Clemmie and Louise make their way into the courtyard and follow their guide towards the metal-studded front door. As they walk, Clemmie gestures to the neighbouring building. "An illustrious past, that one. Number 8, before it was apartments."

"How so?"

"Used to be known as the 'London Cage'."

"Sounds ominous."

"Belonged to MI19, part of the War Office. They tortured captured Germans in there. Most of them talked, too."

Louise waits for Clemmie to struggle up the large stone steps ahead of her. The door creaks open as they approach. Their guide gestures for them to enter, although he remains outside.

*

The interior is abruptly sterile, comprising just a walkthrough metal detector and a large mirror along one wall. Nothing else.

"Bombproof; a blast room?"

Clemmie nods, then approaches the mirror. A narrow aperture slides open. She feeds through their passports, then starts to speak in perfect Russian, to Louise's evident surprise.

"Hello, we are here to see…"

A crackling metallic voice interrupts her from a speaker above the mirror. "First, through the detector."

Clemmie gestures Louise to the machine. "He says to go through."

"In the church, you said you couldn't speak…?"

"Oh, did I?"

The women do as instructed, then the voice crackles back into life. "The stick. Put it on the conveyor."

Once they have passed through security and the appropriate light has switched to green, Clemmie returns to the mirror "As I said, we are here…"

Again, the Russian voice interrupts her: "Leave your coats in the cloakroom, then go through."

Realising that further chit-chat isn't on offer, the two women make their way to a previously concealed door that has now opened within the far wall.

"As friendly as he sounded?"

"We're in. That's all that matters."

*

The cathedral is deserted, aside from the occasional appearance of a lay assistant scuttling between pools of light within the interior darkness as they make the cathedral ready for the upcoming service. Even with his recognition training, Stig finds it hard to tell them apart. They seem to all share the same muted headscarves, pallid skin tones and angular bone structures: as if only marginally different versions of the same batch manufacture. He takes time to explore the interior that stretches out in front of him like a vast empty stage between performances. He draws up one of the small, wooden chairs that have been arranged so carefully around the two side walls, and he breathes in the atmosphere, as well as the stale incense from a previous service. He looks across to the opposite wall and is met by a hundred pairs of painted eyes staring back at him. A mutual assessment. Large, polished marble columns interrupt his line of sight in all directions. They create a forest of shadows that seem to open onto secret glades: distinct, delineated areas of the cathedral that have been set aside for differing uses. There is a lectern with a heavy Bible, perhaps for confessions. A knee-high candle holder runs for several metres up to an imposing freestanding depiction of Jesus on the cross. An area is separated from the nave by an intricate low metal boundary fence, behind which depictions of the Virgin Mary are accompanied by their own dedicated candles. These are backdrops for set-piece rituals he doesn't recognise, in a language he doesn't speak.

When Lev enters, his vestments hide his feet, so he seems to glide across the floor. He spots Stig at once but doesn't immediately approach. Instead, he makes a detour via several icons: crossing himself and offering prayers at each waypoint. Finally, he walks over, then stops, his head cocked inquisitively to one side. "So, you *really* liked the icons? Am I interrupting?"

"No, I'm here alone."

Lev smiles as he takes the neighbouring seat. "Ah, but that is where you're wrong. You are never alone here. He is with you. Close your eyes. Close them." Rather self-consciously, Stig does as requested. "There, do you feel that?"

"What exactly?"

"Calm your mind, relax. Let Him speak to you. As a small voice inside you, perhaps?"

Stig tries again. He scrunches his eyes with more intent than before. He listens attentively, but the silence is interrupted by a loud gurgle from his stomach.

"I think He's hungry."

Lev can't help but laugh. His voice echoes around the interior, breaking the spell and sending the lay assistants back into the shadows. He gets to his feet. "Come on, join me for something to eat, please."

*

Clemmie and Louise stand in a vast, wood-panelled room lined with an imposing collection of Russian art from recent centuries: blustering seascapes alongside huge portraits of ruddy collective farmers. A further room, airier than the first, is visible through a far archway, complete with a large ornate dining table and an exquisite chandelier. No doubt the location for regular ambassadorial receptions. The entire space has been designed to communicate power and geographic scale. The expanse of Russian landscapes and cultures distilled into one room: incontestably vast and diverse. When the man enters, he is, consequently, unimposing, despite his best efforts. Slight, in his fifties, with spectacles, immaculate tailoring and a cold, insipid handshake, he seems to blend with the room rather than compete against it. "Assistant to the Ambassador, Nikolai Ivanovich, at your service."

*

They take the same seats as the night before. Other priests sit together in small rook-like parliaments, or with parishioners, on the other tables around them.

"I have some questions."

"Ah."

"And I was hoping you may be willing to…?"

"Father Igor? If I can."

Stig can see that Lev is disappointed: "What is it?"

"Well, I'd be lying if I said…" He struggles to find the right words. "I had hoped your return visit was for deeper reasons. I had a feeling that you had found something here. Or that something had found you."

Stig slides the piece of paper with the two Latvian surnames across the table. "Do you recognise these members of your congregation?"

"I do, yes."

"We believe they may be worth talking to, about recent events."

"I see. Okay."

"And I'd like you to tell me what you know about each of them."

Lev takes a long time to stare at Stig, watching him closely, with evident compassion and concern. Finally, he sighs and leans forward. "Here's what I'll do." Stig also leans in, so that their faces are just a few inches apart across the table. A quiet conspiracy. "I'll tell you what I know about these people, without compromising myself or them, but in return I want you to do something for me." Stig nods, although with a wary surprise, as Lev continues. "I want you to call on Archangel Michael first. To provide assistance to you during this time."

"But I don't believe, I mean I'm not…"

"Then there's nothing to lose. Think of it as an insurance policy, to make me feel more confident about, well, all this. We'll take this journey together, with one foot in your world, and one foot in mine." Stig leans back with a sigh. "Is that a yes?"

"Fine. If it makes you feel better, yes, fine. Of course."

*

Clemmie and Louise sit behind a large, polished, dark wooden table across from Nikolai Ivanovich. They sip at lemon tea from the finest porcelain.

"Mr Ivanovich."

"Nikolai, please."

"Nikolai, we are here to come to an agreement with you."

"The way you say that; more of a statement than a request."

"We understand you have a team looking into the priest's death."

"And was that a question?"

"It was not. You do."

"And what else do you think you know. Mrs..?"

"Miss. And Clemency, please." He bows his thanks, imbuing even this small gesture with rehearsed diplomatic charm. Clemmie continues: "We know that, on this rare occasion, it's unlikely to be a Kremlin-sanctioned poisoning." Nikolai takes a sip of his tea to hide his ripple of exasperated laughter. "And we know that you're in the dark just as much as we are."

After a sigh, Nikolai reapplies his gracious smile, although with more effort now. "I can confirm that it wasn't us."

"And you've got nothing."

He folds his hands patiently on his lap. "I have every confidence that we will find the culprit. In time."

"And that's exactly what we don't want. This isn't Moscow."

"Yes, the manner in which you are speaking to me suggests we must be in London."

Louise raises her eyebrows just a fraction. She considers interrupting to moderate her boss, as she had done for the priest, but Clemmie is already speaking again. "If it's a criminal matter, we'll brief back to you when justice has been served. Our kind of justice. If it's Russian infighting, you can take it back home and deal with it there. But not here, not in London. And for that kindness on our part, you will stay the hell out of our investigation. That's the agreement."

Nikolai slowly sets aside his cup as if to signal his

intention to speak. "And you think it could be a criminal matter? A robbery that went wrong, perhaps?"

"Perhaps."

He laughs, although evidently with disappointment. His voice is quieter now, with a deeper timbre: "Your passport, on your way in just now, it lit up our system like a Christmas tree. So my security colleagues tell me."

"I made no attempt to conceal myself."

"But someone of your standing, investigating what could be just a criminal matter, however tragic, I think we both know that is rather unlikely. And you are still asking us to trust you?"

"You keep your dogs on a short leash, because if I find them digging around, I'll have them neutered. You can trust me entirely on that."

They stare at each other, unblinking. "I will speak to the Ambassador."

"Do that." She hands over a scrap of paper as she gets to her feet. "I'll be on this number between twelve and one tomorrow. Make sure the Ambassador agrees terms."

*

Having removed the particular icon from the dining hall and placed it on a lectern in the centre of the cathedral, Lev sets about the private service. He has Stig stand at his shoulder, holding a candle, then starts reading relevant sections from the Bible out loud, using the particular sing-song voice he employs exclusively for these occasions. He prays openly, loudly, in both Russian and English, asking for Archangel Michael to bless Stig's ongoing work, as well as to protect him in the name of all that is true. To begin with, Stig simply stands in embarrassed silence. Gradually, however, the two men become more attuned to each other. Stig closes his eyes when he feels it is appropriate, rather than when he is instructed. He finds himself echoing Lev's "amen" at key points. By the time Lev draws a cross in the air above Stig's head, there is no sense that he is an intruder within a foreign religion. He is an active participant. He re-joins the here and now and finds Lev smiling at him.

"That's it."

"Right, good, I mean thank you."

"How about a shot of vodka to help pick yourself up?"

"Wha…seriously?"

"You think priests don't drink? Russian priests? Seriously?!"

*

Standing in the cathedral's makeshift library, the two men knock back a vodka and then take their seats.

"It won't be Andersons."

"What makes you say that?"

"A market gardener. Supplies the cathedral with our flowers. Wonderful man. It won't be him."

"Which leaves Liepins."

"'The little linden tree', from the Latvian."

"And what can you tell me about him? Also, a wonderful man?"

"He's a lawyer." Stig smiles at the incongruity. "A humanitarian lawyer."

"Ah."

"I don't know of his family situation; I've only ever seen him visit alone. A regular worshipper."

"And Father Igor took his confession?"

"Almost exclusively. He said I was too young; Liepins."

"Charming."

"As long as he confesses before God, then who am I to dictate the terms of his relationship with the divine?"

"And did you get the sense that their conversations, Liepins and Father Igor, went beyond just the confessional? Did they drink vodka for example?"

"Orthodoxy is a family. We believe that the Church, in its physical form, is the body of Christ. Yes, he would most definitely have had wider conversations with his spiritual father, about all aspects of his life and the ways in which he could live in a Godlier way, according to the teachings of Jesus."

"Would that have included his legal practice, for example?"

"Certainly. His work is commendable by all accounts."

"But you didn't actually hear them discussing it?"

"No."

"What did you hear?" asks Stig. Lev sighs, unable to bring examples to mind. "Think. Anytime you heard them talking."

"There was once, during Great Lent. We fast then."

"And?"

"They were talking, in the bookshop, just on the other side of this wall here."

"What about?"

"Peace."

"Peace?"

"Yes, peace. Liepins was frustrated by events in Ukraine, I think it was. Or perhaps the Crimean Peninsula specifically."

Stig hides his sudden interest. "Try hard and think back. What did they say, what exactly did you hear?"

"They were equally agitated. Frustrated. They were discussing whether the Church could use its influence in the area. Broadly, that was the thrust of their conversation."

"Thank you. And one final question?"

"Yes, if I can answer, within the boundaries I have already said."

Stig produces a pencil and paper. "Where would I find this Liepins and what does he look like?"

"That's two questions."

"Forgive me."

"Ah, see, you are getting the hang of this! And the good news: Jesus forgives everything."

Stig manages a smirk as Lev begins to draw.

Chapter Fourteen

Louise crosses the road to pick up the man's tail as he leaves his office. Not one of the Golden Circle law firms by any means, but a reputable practice with a suitably grand Cannon Street address. He is older than Lev's crude sketch implies, but the resemblance is unmistakable. Fifties, tall, gaunt, with distinctive grey streaks running along each temple and the Prince of Wales flannel suit that has become his trademark within the legal fraternity. Stig is already ahead of them along the street, in Liepins' direction of travel. Clemmie, who is covering his other possible route, now takes her place at the rear of the surveillance formation, behind Louise.

Liepins opts for a bus from Bank Station, rather than the underground, perhaps to enjoy the buttery evening sunset as it streaks through the gaps between London's high-rises. The number 11, towards Fulham. He is on his way home. On embarking, he takes his seat at the front of the upper deck. Louise follows him up, while Clemmie and Stig cover the three doorways on the lower deck between them.

On reaching Fulham Town Hall, Liepins

disembarks and rounds the first corner down Moore Park Road. Louise continues as team leader, with Stig and Clemmie holding back to take positions at the junction. Liepins pauses outside his Victorian maisonette to fumble for keys within his weathered brown briefcase. Louise has to swerve to avoid him, only to step directly into the path of another pedestrian striding up the road in the opposite direction. "Sorry." She glances up just long enough to catch sight of the other pedestrian's distinctive green eyes before continuing to walk on, trying to avoid drawing any further attention to herself. It is only when she approaches a parking meter that she can credibly stop to tap at its buttons and turn back to resume her surveillance of the target once again. Liepins is now staring at his front door, a key already inserted into the lock although he has yet to turn it. He merely stands there, as if pausing, deep in thought. Perhaps preparing for what he will find on the other side of the threshold? Slowly, he leans his forehead against the door, still without having opened it. Louise continues to watch with an increasing sense of concern. He is just standing there, leaning. Then, she notices she is not the only one watching Liepins. On the opposite side of the street. The pedestrian. Green eyes. Waiting. She starts to run, just as Liepins' legs buckle. She is at a full sprint as he collapses straight down to the floor. The pedestrian, who has also started to recross the street, now sees her. He stops in his tracks, suddenly alert. Stig is also on the move, approaching from a distance. Louise screams in his general direction, as she closes in on Liepins. "No! There. Pedestrian. Green eyes!" The pedestrian is already walking hurriedly in the opposite direction. Louise's shouting spurs him into a run, with Stig giving chase. Clemmie does her best to rush to Louise's assistance; to help bundle Liepins into his house.

Stig rounds the corner, but the pedestrian is nowhere to be seen. Frantically, he runs this way and that, glancing down into the small entrance courtyards of the basement flats he passes, while trying to catch a glimpse of the passengers within each of the many buses that pass in both directions. It is useless; he has lost his quarry.

*

Clemmie manages to move Liepins' legs out of the way so that she can close the front door behind them. Louise drags him deeper into the hallway, finally propping him against the stairs to the first floor. Barely conscious, Liepins takes her hand and guides it to his thigh. He presses it there, urgently.

"There? There, is that it?" She sets about unbuckling his belt and pulling down his trousers. Sure enough, there is a tiny puncture mark at the top of one of the man's thighs.

"Poison. What do I do, suck it out?"

Louise leans down to start to try and extract the toxin from the small hole, but Clemmie beats her back with her stick. "No! Christ knows what it is."

Stig enters to find a half-naked man lolling around the floor with Louise about to suck at his leg and Clemmie hitting her with a stick. He hesitates just for a second, "Right," then closes the door behind him and races through the flat. "Hello, is anyone home? Hello?"

Liepins grabs violently at Louise's hair. Clemmie resorts to falling onto his arm to try and break his grip, but he won't let go. He pulls Louise close to his face as he gasps for breath and whispers hoarsely into her ear, "A woman."

"On the street? It was a man, green eyes, he did this?"

"Sokolova. The source. Protect her." And with that, Liepins slumps into a final stillness.

Chapter Fifteen

Clemmie storms into the wood-panelled interior as fast as her stick will allow her. Nikolai is already waiting for her with his rehearsed smile. "Clemency, how lovely to…"

She surges through the room and right up to his face. She spits out her words in Russian: "I said call them off!" He tries to quieten her with cooing noises rather than actual words. Clemmie can now see why; a reception is underway in the grand room beyond a nearby arch. "Answer, or I scream the bloody house down!"

Nikolai urges her to come with him in the opposite direction. "Of course, of course, this way please."

"And take your bloody hands off me!"

*

The refined sounds of a rarefied reception can be heard through the walls. Nikolai accepts two glasses of champagne from a waiter who appears at the door, then returns to his seat opposite Clemmie. "To our enduring relations."

She doesn't return his toast. "What d'you think

you are doing?"

"Perhaps I should have said to our enduring *civil* relations?"

"I will come after you personally for this."

Nikolai sighs heavily. "Well, then perhaps you'd best tell me what it is that I am supposed to have done?"

"Oh, don't give me that. Hypodermic. On an umbrella, was it? This isn't bloody Le Carré!"

Nikolai examines the streams of tiny bubbles in his glass, then sips at the champagne with due reverence. "It would seem that the only comparison…is that they are both fiction?"

The reality begins to dawn on Clemmie that she may be in the wrong. She gulps at her own drink to hide her rising concern. His stare is a mix of anger, but also inevitability. "You may have been a little premature in blaming the Russians, as seems to be your national habit, very sadly."

"How many are on your investigations team?"

"Two. They arrived from Moscow."

"Green eyes?"

"I beg your pardon?"

"Do either of them have green eyes?"

Nikolai slowly gets to his feet and walks to the corner of the room. He straightens his tie, then reaches for an old-fashioned internal telephone and speaks so that Clemency can hear every word of his call: "Send in our colleagues, the new arrivals." There is a pause. Clemmie can hear the muffled concern from the other end of the line. "Yes, I am quite sure. Send them in to me now. On my authority."

Nikolai replaces the receiver and retakes his seat in silence. An awkward minute later, there is a knock at the door and two men enter. Broad shoulders, short hair, ill-fitting suits and unforgiving hands. They shuffle by the door, awaiting instructions. Nikolai grandly gestures for Clemmie to look in their direction. One is grey-eyed, the other brown.

"Dmitry, where have the pair of you been all day? In English please, so there can be no further misunderstandings."

By his artless demeanour, it is clear that Dmitry is resistant to transparency of any kind. "I think, sir, it would be best if you introduced us first?"

Nikolai fires him a stare. "I said *where*?"

"At our desks."

"Working on?"

Again, Dmitry struggles to get the words out. "Working on the Father Igor case. As are our instructions, from *Moscow*, sir." The location designation emphasised, as if to pull rank.

"And have you left your desks today, Tima, either of you?"

The other man looks at his feet as he shuffles on the spot. "Only now for the reception. The Ambassador said that it was permitted, sir?"

"Thank you, that will be all."

The two men leave, as confused as when they entered. Clemmie cannot meet Nikolai's gaze. She places both hands on the table in front of her, palms down. "I owe you an apology."

"Yes."

"I am sincerely sorry."

"More."

"That I…" She looks up in the hope that he isn't serious.

"More!"

"I am sincerely sorry that I screwed this up so spectacularly."

"Good." Seemingly happy, Nikolai leans back and resumes the aesthetic appreciation of his champagne. "You know, Clemency, I can't help feeling that our two countries would be a lot closer if you occasionally gave us the benefit of the doubt."

She shrugs at the strange turn of the conversation: "Maybe."

"I'm sure of it. Just think, if we joined forces again, like in the Second World War, we could focus on what unites us, not always what divides us."

Clemmie senses a subtext but can't define it. "You

sided with Hitler, if I'm not mistaken?"

"You see, there you go again. But ultimately, we paid our debt, did we not? An unimaginable price." She shrugs her agreement. "So, in the interests of building this partnership, I am prepared to trust your methods in favour of dear Dmitry's for a further twenty-four hours. To give you the benefit of the doubt. As a courtesy, because this is your city, as you seemed at such pains to tell me before. How does that sound?"

"Generous, considering."

"But that is as long as I can keep my dogs, as you call them, behind a desk. After that, they will grow frustrated and need exercising."

"I understand."

"Good." He raises his glass once again. "Then, to our enduring *civil* relations?"

This time she raises her glass in reply.

*

Clemmie re-enters the flat with little enthusiasm. She traipses up the stairs and finds Stig, equally disheartened, cleaning the toilet. "She won?"

"Story of my life."

Clemmie moves through to the bedroom. Louise is busy working on the storyboard, using red thread to link the photographs of the deceased: the priest, the wet worker and now the lawyer. Clemmie slumps into a nearby chair and produces a bottle of vodka from her coat. "Stole it from the embassy."

"Well, when in a kleptocracy…"

"Indeed. Want some?"

Louise finds three paper cups but heads over to Clemmie brandishing only two. "We'll let him finish up first, eh?" They exchange a conspiratorial smile as Louise takes a seat and Clemmie pours. "What did he say?"

"It wasn't them."

"Oh, sure! And nor was Salisbury?"

"I think he was telling the truth."

"Ouch."

"Yup, ouchski."

They stare at the photos of death in front of them.

"A man with green eyes and a woman called Sokolova. That's all we've got."

"Yup."

Stig enters, still wearing his pink Marigold gloves. Louise welcomes him with a snort of laughter.

"Why the smile?"

"Well look at him, he looks like a trans dinner lady."

Clemmie gestures to the storyboard. "I meant the priest. Why the smile?"

Stig finds the extra cup and pours himself a

double. "As a message?"

"Okay, but to whom?"

"Anyone who saw the photo. In the papers. On the news."

"And how often do the mainstream networks show pictures of corpses? Never."

Still with his pink gloves on and vodka in hand, Stig follows her line of sight, as well as her line of thinking. "So the killer must've known they'd get coverage ahead of the hit?"

Louise is now also more serious: "Which means the distribution channel was either involved, or accounted for."

Clemmie struggles to her feet and leads them into the main room. "If we find where it was broadcast, we find the next link in the chain."

Stig is first to his laptop. "What am I searching for?"

"'Smiling priest', 'dead priest with a smile', anything like that. Who used the picture?"

He pulls away his gloves with his teeth as he types, then regrets it as he considers where they have been. He carries on regardless. "Just one site."

"Go on?'

"Latvian."

"No shit. Show me."

He spins his laptop to reveal a current affairs

journal in Riga. Clemmie peers at the photo of the dead priest across its front page. "What does the headline say? Can you translate that?" The text refreshes: *Suspected NATO informant dead in London.*

Louise squeezes between them. "NATO? Says who?"

Stig searches the article, but there is no attributed journalist. "Must be a cut-and-paste job. Maybe if I search the first paragraph?" He copies the article's introductory text and searches again. A slew of articles appears, all from locations within Eastern Europe and the Baltic states. They share elements of the Latvian copy, as well as differing crops of the same photo.

Clemmie seems unsurprised. "And none of them are recognisable media outlets. They're all pop-ups?"

"Unattributed, but everywhere. What next?"

"Go back in time, who posted first? The Latvians?"

Finally free of his gloves, Stig taps away hurriedly. Louise is the first to see the name of a British newspaper as the page refreshes again. "The original text, but no photo. Look at the location of the paper. They're based around the corner."

Stig stops his tapping. "They'll have sent a reporter straight round when the police turned up in force."

Clemmie is evidently less convinced. "So, this is all above board, is it?"

"The rebroadcasters just copied the story. That's totally possible."

"And the original, does it mention NATO?"

Stig checks. "No."

Louise reaches over Stig's shoulder and clicks back to the Latvian article. "An anti-NATO spin is hardly surprising for the region though. They would have added it as a matter of course."

"And the photo?"

"Also kosher. Their press get to print crime scene photos. It's a cultural thing."

They fall into silence as they each wrestle with the available facts. The photo of the dead priest stares out from Stig's laptop screen, smiling at their evident confusion. Clemmie suddenly straightens, as if literally hit by the idea. "Hang on." As if in a trance, she heads back to the storyboard.

"What? What is it?"

"Bring your laptop."

Stig and Louise follow. As they enter the bedroom, Clemmie is already examining the photos of Father Igor. "Notice anything?"

They look to the storyboard, then back to the Latvian article's photo. Stig then holds the laptop up beside the wall to make a closer comparison. "It's different."

Sure enough, there are tiny variances between the

online photo and those on the wall. Clemmie speaks quietly, lost in thought again. "But these are the only ones in the police file. We have them all." She retakes a seat, downs the last of her vodka and rests her chin on her stick in front of her, deep in thought.

Stig is about to speak, then stops himself and rethinks his ideas. He finally ventures, "So, this one...wasn't taken by forensics, but by the killer."

Louise nods along with his points. "Who must have leaked it to the press. It could only have come from them."

Stig retakes the baton. "We just need to ask them for the source."

They turn to Clemmie for her approval, but it isn't forthcoming. "Maybe. But let's just look at this from every possible angle. Go back to the beginning. The original story. What did it say, exactly?"

Stig rechecks the English article. "Just that a priest has been found dead, nothing about NATO."

"Dead, but not murdered?"

"No."

Louise steps in. "The journalist wouldn't presuppose. It's only murder if the coroner says so."

"And the smile?"

Stig skim-reads once again. "Nothing."

"Louise? Think laterally. C'mon."

"Okay, the smile was deemed as unnecessarily

upsetting for the family, by the editor most likely."

"And why else might you choose not to report it, Stig?"

"If you didn't want to draw attention to it. At least, not to the UK audience."

"Right, because it wasn't intended for them. Also possible."

Louise remains unconvinced. "That's pure speculation."

Clemmie seems pleased. She is going to have to do better if she wants to pass Louise's evidence threshold. Stig taps at his laptop as she takes her time before speaking again. "Okay, there's another possible explanation." Louise crosses her arms in anticipation. "The journalist didn't get the photo from a leak."

Louise laughs openly at the idea. "Oh right, now you're clutching. The journalist's the murderer? I don't think so. Let's go back to where we were: it was leaked."

Clemmie is about to try another scenario when she notices Stig's wide-eyed reaction to his screen: "What is it?"

"Who."

He reveals his find: the article. The journalist's name: Maxim Kuzmin. Stig clicks. A photo begins to download. The journalist's headshot. Black hair. Cropped. Black eyebrows. Distinctive green eyes staring back at them. Louise turns to face the others with a new intensity; her role as dissenter already forgotten. "It's him."

Chapter Sixteen

Maxim Kuzmin sits tucked away in the corner of the large, open-plan office, nursing his tea, as the editorial conference goes on around him. The editor – a fearsome man, as they always are – is holding forth about the particular stories that will form Sunday's front page. Another royal abuse allegation has been chosen as the splash. The editor's hatred of the royal family is visceral. "It'd be more of a story if a royal *wasn't* debauched these days, wouldn't it? Inbred dog-humping Gollums, the lot of them." Maxim tunes out. There will be a few minutes' more ranting before the meeting can resume and they will plan out the rest of the paper, carefully distributing the heavyweight stories and opinions among the tittle-tattle in the earnest belief that people still enjoy the holistic editorial curation of a newspaper, rather than the vacuous bite-sized nuggets available on their handheld devices.

He surveys his various colleagues: a broad split of ages, ethnicities and educations; the antithesis of the McMedia titles that now dominate the UK media landscape, with their overtly political proprietors and barely concealed biases. Here, in this room, are the happy few who manage to sustain a daily distaste for vested interests and file copy without fear or favour. The title, and its bombastic republican editor, have been good to Maxim. They have provided him with the room needed to develop his own ideas and agendas, for which he is both thankful and loyal. At least, until now. But now he is answering to a higher calling that he knows may ultimately cost the paper, and his colleagues, their reputations. He feels the responsibility keenly, but it does not blunt his conviction. After all, it is simply a matter of time. The rise of the internet, coupled with diminishing advertising spends, means that their days are already numbered. His actions will simply act as an accelerant to the approaching flames. Consequently, his current relationship with the title is purely functional: a convenient vessel in which to carry the narratives and messages that serve the wider plan: *her* plan. And what a plan. If the title is to perish, let it be gloriously for this cause, in one final audacious act for peace, rather than as a whimper at the hands of the inevitable creditors and receivers.

"Maxim?"

"Sorry, what?"

All eyes are on him.

"If you would be so kind as to pay us a little of your attention?"

"Of course, sorry."

"The Latvian story? Any developments for this weekend?"

"Well, maybe, yes, as it happens."

"And will you be sharing them, or am I expected to be telepathic now?"

"The priest."

"The dead one?"

"Yes. It seems he was working for NATO on the quiet."

"NATO? As in NATO?"

"Yes."

The skin at the editor's temples begins to pulse as he considers the implications. "Here in London?"

"Yes."

"Doing what?"

"Inciting."

"Inciting?"

"Part of a network in London."

"Have they no shame?"

"NATO, or the priesthood?"

"All of them! Can you stand something up by Sunday?"

"Yes, I think so."

"Take them to the cleaners." He turns back to the rest of the room. "Well, that's page four sorted. No, make it three. Now Helen, you've got an update on the gas pipeline into Germany?" But Maxim has already stopped listening again. He has what he needs.

*

Back at his desk, Maxim ensures that his screen is not visible to the rest of the room, before logging on using a dark-web portal. He dons a headset as he waits for the connection to establish itself. A woman's face soon fills the screen. Thin, crimson lips. Jet eyes. A precise manner. Maxim speaks quietly, without any preamble. "This weekend."

"Making the link to the Alliance?"

"And the lawyer, too."

"Good." She sips at an espresso. "And the next name?"

"There isn't. I mean, there were other people around him."

Her eyes narrow over her drink. "What kind of other people?"

"Organised."

"So, they are onto you?"

"Not that I know of. Onto him maybe."

She takes her time to think things through. "If you have been careless?"

"I haven't."

"We need the next name. The chain: it must go on, all the way."

"I will find a way."

"We are relying on you."

The feed is cut from her end, but her words linger in his ears. They are relying on him. She is. There is no greater feeling. More than just a journalist, he is now a vital part, albeit a small part, but a *vital* part in her plan. He opens his word-processing software and enters his article's headline: '*Second NATO agitator found dead*'.

Chapter Seventeen

A Bored, young promotions man stands outside the newspaper's main office, handing out samples of bottled water to each passer-by. With the prospect of the stuffy rush-hour underground ahead of them, the evening commuters readily accept his free offerings. Maxim's green eyes make him distinctive even from a distance, and Stig has plenty of time to reach into the back of his cooler to retrieve the particular bottle. He feels the weight lift from his hand as Maxim passes by, all the while making sure to look the other way to avoid eye contact. Only when Maxim is further down the road and out of sight do Clemmie and Louise appear at Stig's side. Louise brandishes her mobile phone on which an icon can be seen traversing a digital London map. "He's past the underground. Now stationary."

"A bus stop?"

Louise strokes at the small screen to zoom in. A bus stop icon. She clicks to reveal the route. "Destination: Fulham."

Clemmie smiles at the predictability of his behaviour. "Of course you are."

"He's going back to Liepins' flat."

*

Having finished his water, Maxim leaves the empty bottle on the seat beside him and exits the bus. He makes his way back onto Moore Park Road and then passes the maisonette to establish that the location is both empty and free from prying eyes before heading to the back of the property. Having ducked under the plastic washing line, he sets about a window and gains easy access to the kitchen. Once inside, with gloved hands, he begins a fingertip search of every cupboard and drawer, being careful to create a minimum of disturbance and noise.

Finding nothing of interest in the kitchen, Maxim edges his way down the hallway and into the lounge. The interior is sparse and functional: the bachelor pad of a man who doesn't – didn't – spend much time at home. Aside from the expected books on law and a noticeable collection on international relations and the politics of Eastern Europe, there is little else to draw Maxim's attention. He heads back to the hallway to climb the stairs. Just then, there is a sudden noise from the kitchen. The sound of a door. Maxim immediately backs up to the wall. He waits for a further sound, but there is just silence from the kitchen's gloomy interior. He eases his way along the hallway, slowly, inch by inch, then surges into the kitchen. He comes face-to-face with the second intruder: Liepins' cat, which has appeared to protest loudly at the lack of food. Sure enough, there is a cat flap at the bottom of the kitchen's exterior door.

"Little bastard."

To quieten the animal, rather than out of any compassion, Maxim finds some biscuits and refills the cat's bowl. The loud meowing is soon replaced by a more agreeable sound of eating and purring. Maxim heads back into the hallway and climbs the stairs.

*

The first floor comprises a small bathroom and two bedrooms. Unusually, the master bedroom has been set aside as a home office, and the second, much smaller room as the cramped sleeping quarters. Maxim starts with this second room. There is a single bed, a cupboard with a collection of Prince of Wales checked suits and very little else. He moves on to the expansive study. Quite clearly, this is the room in which Liepins spent the majority of his time when at home. A central antique mahogany writing desk dominates the space, complete with a freestanding computer on the green leather insert. There is a sense of theatre to the layout, indicating the degree to which Liepins regarded the status of his own work.

The walls are dotted with similarly self-aggrandising legal parchments that reveal his many and varied qualifications in all aspects of humanitarian law. A sumptuous Oriental rug and dark wooden bookshelf complete the look.

Maxim takes his time to examine each of the desk's drawers in turn. He flicks through the diaries, address books and assorted legal notebooks with the attention of a trained journalist. Every entry is assessed, every name noted. Next, he examines the box files that have been arranged on the bookcase's lower shelf. They are all carefully named, in alphabetical order, according to specific legal cases relating to former Soviet Socialist Republics: Armenia, Azerbaijan, Belarus, Estonia, Georgia and the rest. He pulls at one of the files but is unable to remove it. On closer examination, he sees the metal bar that has been fitted across the bookshelf to stop just such an attempt. The bar is attached firmly by a padlock at each end of the heavy wooden frame. Unperturbed, he heads back into the bedroom and retrieves the duvet from the single bed and uses it to cover the entire bookshelf, as a baffle. One strike of his heel is enough to send the metal bar to the floor with the sound duly muffled. He pauses to ensure there are no follow-up noises of concern from the neighbouring houses or the street outside, before continuing with his work. He takes the file marked 'Georgia' and carefully examines its contents. A case relating to war crimes comprising both written and photographic evidence of ethnic cleansing in South Ossetia. References to a previous allegation in Abkhazia. He replaces the file and reaches for 'Latvia'. This time he spreads the paperwork out on the desk in front of him, so he can scan multiple documents at the same time. He finds references to NATO and studies these paragraphs in greater detail. One name is repeated across the various papers. A woman's name. He reaches into his pocket for his notebook and adds the name to his list. He continues reading. Another reference to NATO, and another name. This time a man's. Another note. He repeats this process until all the pages have been examined, before returning the file to the shelf.

Next, he searches the rest of the room for any other miscellaneous clues. Behind the framed pictures, under the desk and carpet, behind each desk drawer. Once the entire room has been deconstructed, then reconstructed, he goes back to the bookcase and surveys the damage. Having considered his options, he removes the retaining bar entirely, then uses a pen from the desk to apply black ink to the cracks in the wood as a make-do camouflage over the splintered areas. He then carefully collects up any chips of wood from the floor and pockets these before remaking the bed in the small room. Finally, carrying the metal bar with him, he descends to the hallway. He rounds the bottom of the stairs and heads for the kitchen…and straight into Stig's fast-approaching fist.

*

The cat pads Maxim back into consciousness as it tests his viability as a pillow. Suitably impressed, it curls up on the sofa next to him and falls sound asleep. He feels the restraints as he comes to. The plastic washing line has been used to bind his hands and feet. Clemmie and Louise are perched in front of him. He can hear Stig's breathing to his rear, seated close behind the sofa. His green eyes blink open, then come to rest on Louise: "Hello again."

She meets his stare with a smile. "If you shout, then the neighbours may call the police. As a three-times murderer, you probably don't want that. So, stay quiet."

"I don't know what you are…"

Stig simultaneously clasps Maxim's mouth with one hand and hits him hard across the back of the head with the other. The result is all of the intended pain, but with none of the correlating noise. "Don't even go there."

The cat decides that Maxim isn't living up to expectations and leaves the room. Louise waits for Maxim to return his attention to her before continuing, "You killed the priest on demand, with a smile. Who for?"

"Wrong. I didn't kill him. Now, who are you?"

"Who did?"

"Answer *my* question."

This gets him another muzzling and beating from Stig. Louise waits patiently again until he comes to. "Who did?"

"A woman. Professional."

"But you killed her, and the owner of this flat, why?"

Maxim looks around him with a frustrated sigh, seemingly as much for the inconvenience as for the pain. Stig raises his hand again, but Louise gestures for him to wait. Maxim struggles to turn so as to speak to Stig: "Go ahead. But you won't stop her. Too late. Nothing you can do now."

Intrigued, Louise steps closer. "Who do you think we are?"

"A wild stab in the dark. The cavalry. All the way from Riga."

Louise turns to Clemmie with narrowed eyes.

"So here I am. Prosecute me. Go on. Let's have this out in court. Let's let the whole world hear what the hell you've been doing." The others share a smile, which just makes Maxim even more impassioned. "Smile, that's it, just like the priest. Smile all the way as she takes you down!"

Louise winces at the sudden increase in the volume of Maxim's voice. She gives Stig a nod. He immediately seizes Maxim's head once again from behind and covers his mouth and nose. Maxim wrestles for air, but Stig's grip is unshakeable. Louise steps closer to whisper into his ear, "I said no shouting. There's a good murderer."

Gradually, Maxim's face turns from red to a deep purple as the lack of oxygen becomes critical. Only now does Clemmie get to her feet and join Louise. She makes certain that he, Maxim, is looking directly at her before he gives Stig the signal to release his grip. Maxim doesn't take his eyes off his saviour as he lurches for air. She waits for him to regain his composure. "Now you listen to me. We aren't NATO, I've never been to Riga, and whatever you think you know is wrong. Gottit?" He nods. "Good. But we won't think twice about handing you over to NATO unless you start telling us what we need to know. And that's all you're getting. So, don't blow this chance. Clear?"

Maxim surveys the three of them, then takes his time to consider his realistic options. "I want immunity from prosecution."

Clemmie blinks back in her astonishment. "Come again?"

"For what I know. Immunity."

"It's not ours to give."

"Ah! You're not official then?"

Without a moment's hesitation, Clemmie gestures to Stig. The grip is reinstated, and Maxim's eyes soon bulge once again with a potent blend of fear and desperation. Clemmie remains entirely calm as he struggles in front of her. "I told you, don't blow this. You want to play games, or get out of this mess? So, play nicely, yes?" Another nod, another signal from Clemmie and Stig's grip re-releases. Maxim splutters as he sucks urgently at the room around him. Small pressure-welts have started to appear in the skin around his nostrils. Clemmie examines them sympathetically before stepping back to look deep into his green eyes once again. "So, tell me."

"The Russians."

The mood in the room shifts. Maxim can sense Clemmie's interest has been piqued.

"What about them?"

"They will give me immunity."

"Is that right?"

"My mother. I qualify for citizenship. I want that. Citizenship and immunity."

"Let me get this straight, you want us to hand you over to the Russians, whose priest you killed?"

"I didn't kill him!"

"As a favour for talking to us?"

"Immunity for cooperation. Yes."

Stig leans close to Maxim's ear but speaks to Clemmie. "Leave me alone with him. He'll talk alright."

Clemmie is evidently in two minds. "And what would we tell the Russians? To arrange this. What's your bait?"

"The next war. How to stop war. That's what I have to trade."

*

The diplomatic car drives past the maisonette's front door and pulls over farther down Moor Park Road. Two men get out. Despite the darkness, the breadth of their shoulders reveals they are the two Muscovites from the Embassy: Dmitry and the other "dog", Tima. They walk up and down the street before gesturing for the car to reverse. Tima then opens the car's rear door and ushers the male passenger towards Louise, who is waiting in the building's dark entrance. Nikolai steps past her and into the hallway where Clemmie greets him. He gestures around as he whispers fiercely: "The address of the murder victim? Have you lost your mind?! Have you any idea how this would look if it got into the press?"

"Well, he is a journalist."

Nikolai double-takes, unsure of whether she is joking. When he realises she isn't, he pivots and heads straight back towards the front door. Clemmie reaches after him with the crook of her stick. "Woah, hang on."

"This is too much. And to think I trusted you?!"

"I said if it was infighting, it was your mess to clean up. Well, didn't I? So, stop complaining."

Nikolai looks to Dmitry and Tima for their opinion. To Clemmie's evident pleasure, Dmitry shrugs his acceptance of the situation, as if this is quite a normal situation for their line of work.

Clemmie gestures to the door to the main room. "Five minutes. Hear him out. Make up your own mind."

Still evidently unhappy, Nikolai nods them in. "Not a second longer."

*

Nikolai enters to find Maxim still on the sofa, with Stig whispering menacing threats into his ear. Louise and Clemmie retake their seats. Dmitry and Tima opt to stand, one by the entrance, the other by the curtained window. Nikolai takes his time to pull up a chair in front of Maxim and make himself comfortable: a clear signal this conversation will take place on his terms. Finally, he looks up at the journalist and studies him with impassive eyes: "You speak Russian?"

"No. But I speak of Russia."

Nikolai rolls his eyes at the wordplay. "Let me be very clear with you. You are, I am told, responsible for the death of Father Igor."

Maxim fires an accusatory stare at Clemmie, but

Nikolai ignores it. "A Russian citizen and someone I had the great pleasure of knowing as a friend. It is in that context that you are speaking to me now. Please choose your words very carefully."

"He was a collaborator. Your priest-friend."

Nikolai breaths in slowly and deeply through his nose. "Oh dear, we don't seem to be getting off to the best start, do we?" He gestures towards Dmitry, who immediately steps forward while retrieving a Taser from his pocket. Stig removes his hands as the Russian drives the device into Maxim's chest and initiates the electrical current. Despite the plastic bindings, Maxim writhes violently on the sofa in silent pain. Dmitry finishes his work and then steps back to his original position by the door. Nikolai waits for Maxim to return to full consciousness before continuing: "As I was saying, please choose your words very carefully. You killed the priest. Yes, or no?"

"No."

"But you were involved in some way with his death?"

"The planning. But I didn't administer the poison. She did that."

"She?"

"Hired for the purpose. Professional."

"Were you there when he died?"

"Yes."

"So, you watched him die?"

"He was collaborating with NATO, to start a war."

Dmitry steps forward but Nikolai gestures for him to wait. "I asked you a direct question."

"I couldn't have saved him at that stage, even if I'd wanted to."

Nikolai nods to himself but remains poker-faced. "A collaborator. I'd like you to expand on that."

"Not without assurances. Citizenship and immunity. In writing."

Another heavy sigh from the diplomat. "I promise you, these two men will get whatever information I want from you, with no pieces of paper involved. Just electricity."

"I will give you everything. The who, what and how. Here in London, in Riga and in Moscow."

The silence is palpable as it echoes around the room. "Moscow?"

"The Kremlin." Tima lets out an involuntary whistle. Nikolai and Dmitry share a look, as do the others in various combinations. "But for immunity. Citizenship and immunity. Because at some stage you will want me to go public with what I know. You will need me on your side, officially."

"My side? You mean Russia?"

"I mean the side of peace."

"As opposed to the other side which is?"

"Full-scale war along your southwestern border."

Again, Maxim's words hang in the air. Nikolai turns to Clemmie for a silent meeting of minds. She gives him the slightest nod. Nikolai turns back to Maxim: "We will take you as far as the Embassy in the first instance. If your debriefing makes you as invaluable as you say, then we may be prepared to discuss the future."

"Fine. Agreed."

"But if these two gentlemen find that even one sentence of your story doesn't check out, they will be very disappointed."

Maxim is in no doubt that this is a threat. "I understand."

Nikolai exchanges a few words of Russian with Dmitry and Tima, who then cut away Maxim's ties and lead him out. Nikolai slowly gets to his feet, returns the chair to its original position, cleans it of prints, then turns to face Clemmie. "And in return?"

"We want a recording of the debrief. Unedited."

He smiles knowingly at the qualifier at the end of Clemmie's sentence. "Of course. And thereby you will know that you can also trust me. I meant what I said before. We will have to find a way to unite in the end." He nods his appreciation to them all, then quietly leaves without looking back.

*

The diplomatic car steers to the back of the Russian Embassy and down into a discreet subterranean driveway. Dmitry and Tima waste no time in manhandling Maxim from the boot and dragging him into a metal tradesman's lift. They press to go down. The doors close and they begin their descent.

Chapter Eighteen

The next morning, they are at their laptops. Clemmie sits at the middle of the table, with Stig and Louise at either end. The others' conversation ping-pongs over and around her. Stig sighs repeatedly as he works: "Sokolova. She could be anywhere."

Louise is similarly underwhelmed by the task. "There are literally thousands of them."

"And anyway, the other two – a priest and a lawyer – who would've ever put them together?"

Back to Louise. "She could be anyone; any profession."

Clemmie slaps the table with frustration: "Enough! Let's just break this down and start at the beginning."

"Right, and where would that be? Riga?"

"Or London?"

"Moscow maybe? All the Sokolovas in Moscow? Sure, that seems reasonable."

"Enough I said! Let's maybe start with…" She is interrupted by the buzzing of her mobile phone. "Oh, just what we need." She accepts the call with clear trepidation. "Yes. Yes, that's right. Understood. On my way." She gets to her feet, "I've been summoned," and gives an imploring look back to the others as she leaves. "Just see if you can be constructive while I'm gone?"

"You can count on it."

"Constructive's our middle name."

"Which would be a lot easier to search than Sokolova."

*

The Chief's watery blue eyes are as cold as the riverside breeze. Clemmie approaches and leans over the concrete flood defence, choosing to look across the grey water to Westminster Palace rather than meet his gaze.

"Our embassy watchers saw him enter. Late last night. The journalist."

"Yes, I was aware of that."

"And leave this morning on the first flight to Moscow."

"I see."

"You see, but you didn't know that?"

"His trade was for citizenship. They clearly liked his product." She can feel his cool eyes boring into her. "What is it, sir? Specifically?"

"Well, enlighten me, Clemency, because I'm evidently not seeing things the way you are. From my perspective, it looks very much like you've just given away your star asset."

"We have an agreement."

"With the Russians? And you're saying that to reassure me?"

She nods, which prompts a further snarl from the Chief. "I said I wanted usable intelligence *ahead* of them, not a bloody agreement *with* them. What are you thinking?" He reaches for his pipe to calm himself. Different from Whitstable. Longer stemmed. A *Bing's favourite*, on account of it having been Bing Crosby's preference.

Clemmie takes her chance to lead the conversation. "He has information about a ploy to manufacture a conflict, in one of the breakaways."

"By whom?"

"NATO, he says."

"You mean NATO, as in our own side, that NATO?" He tries to light his pipe, but the match blows out in the wind. He throws the entire matchbox away in frustration. "If he is telling the truth, you have just handed the West's entire regional strategy to the other side. I have understood you right, yes?"

"I said a manufactured conflict: confected."

"I heard you the first time!"

"Well, I can't imagine that going hot on the Russian border is the current NATO plan, unless you know otherwise, sir?"

"And there's no need for that tone!"

Clemmie pulls her jacket tighter around her shoulders and turns back to face the view. The Chief finally grumbles his acquiescence: "As mad as some of them are, a third world war isn't currently on the table, no."

"So, we're dealing with another actor. Neither NATO, nor the Russians."

"Yes, I do get your point."

"And my assessment, therefore, taking into account the available evidence, is that we want Moscow in the same thermonuclear tent as us at this precise moment. Unless you think otherwise, sir?"

"I said I take your point." They both take a moment to calm down. "Thoughts?"

"Local nationalists trying to trigger wider tensions. Contractors wanting to sell more hardware. Maybe the Chinese just stirring things up. Christ knows."

"None of them particularly desirable."

"Not when you add in the Kremlin and NATO. Or, at least, factions from both."

"So, you do believe him?"

"As do our Russian friends seemingly."

"I don't like it. Dealing with the Reds, it never ends well." Clemmie gives him a look. "Sorry, you know that better than most." He lights his pipe, this time using an old copper Zippo retrieved from the depths of a jacket pocket. "And what happens if they renege on the deal, have you considered that?"

"Of course. But we have a piece of the jigsaw they don't. A name."

"The next name? As in a daisy chain?"

"It would seem so."

He grumbles his reluctant admiration as he puffs the embers into life. "Well, that's something I suppose."

"Quite a big something, I thought." He gives her the faintest of smiles. "So, I have your permission to continue? Sir?"

"To stop a war, yes, alright."

"Good. I'll get back to what I was doing then, shall I?"

He waves her away with a murmur, and she walks off. Within just a few strides, her phone rings once again. She checks the number and turns to call back to the Chief. "It's them." But he has already gone.

Clemmie re-enters the flat brandishing a USB drive. The other two are still failing spectacularly in their attempts to find the right Sokolova.

"Here we go."

"From the Embassy?"

Clemmie nods as she plugs it into Louise's laptop. "Scrub it first."

Louise sets about running her various antivirus programmes. "He kept his word. Honest Russians, whatever next?"

"They flew him to Moscow. Maxim. This morning."

Stig makes his way around to Louise's end of the table. "Let's see what he was trading."

Louise gets the all-clear from her system: the USB is clean. She clicks the video file. The screen opens to reveal Maxim in a small, soundproofed room, shackled to a metal table, across from Dmitry. Tima prowls around in the shadows, lending an unsettling air to events. The debrief is in its early stages – the establishing questions – so Louise scrolls forward, to a more animated section of the conversation. Dmitry is now leaning in, menacingly close to Maxim. "Say that again, slowly,"

"He was a price worth paying."

The Russian suddenly lunges, and grabs hold of Maxim. He pulls him close and drives his forehead into the journalist's nose. Blood splashes across the table in a viscous crescent. "Really! Was he? Says who, you?!"

Maxim, bloodied and shaken, is spluttering a reply as the second blow strikes him. This time, from behind. Maxim's face crashes down onto the table and a tooth shoots off out of frame.

Louise pours herself more tea. "Don't mess around, do they?"

Maxim manages to sit back up in his chair. He spits his words out, coated in blood: "You think it's better to do nothing? To let them start a war, directed by Riga? The psychological operations cell? Is that better?"

This gets Dmitry's attention. He leans back to allow Maxim to continue uninterrupted. "Go on."

"It's how they do it, don't you see? Grey operations. Getting the Church to do their bidding. The priest; fermenting unrest. Then the lawyer; making allegations. Questions in The Hague. Lies in the press. Constantly undermining. Chipping away at the stability of a country. Inciting the youth. Until, voila, you have the next Maidan or Arab spring on your hands. You want that?"

"You said directed by Riga?"

"Of course! Then NATO gets to ride in on a white horse and take over. Proclaiming that they're the solution, not the cause. The antidote to their own lies."

Dmitry shakes his head disdainfully: "You have murdered for a conspiracy."

"No! They are doing it. We have people who know, from that world. Specialists. On our side now." He knows he is losing the Russian, his voice grows more desperate. "They help us to recognise the signs. Of the PsyOps cell. Believe me! They're there for God's sake, in Latvia, you can go see the building for yourself!"

"What I see is a murderer."

"You see nothing. We used their own techniques against them. A story here in the newspaper, an accusation there on a blog. And you know what? They responded. In real-time. We could see it all. The institutions that were speaking on Riga's behalf, spinning their lines, creating division. Charities. Broadcasters. Think Tanks. Doing NATO's dirty work."

Dimitry's tone changes, to that of a father speaking with an errand child. "And who is this 'we'?"

"The Swarm."

"The what?"

"The Swarm."

Louise gives Stig a smirk as they watch the screen. "Sounds like something from Marvel."

Maxim wipes away the blood from his mouth using his shoulder before resuming his story. "We are a collection of the like-minded. Information warriors. From the same places that NATO recruits. The media. Former military. Politicians. Lawyers. People who believe in peace and who are prepared to defend it."

Now it's Stig's turn to roll his eyes. "An army of geeks, oh great."

Maxim continues: "We refuse to be led into conflict again with sexed-up documents and bullshit media stories. We can see what they're doing. You know it. We all do. Creating conflicts for oil, or mining interests, or for God knows what other reasons. Why should we accept that? Why shouldn't we push back? Fight back even?"

Dmitry nods supportively: "Continue."

"So, we doubled down. We targeted these distributors. Embarrassing the institutions that were amplifying Riga's lies. They didn't like it. They got scared that their lackeys were being compromised. And you know what they did?"

Dmitry is taken aback by the sudden question. He regroups quickly. "No, what did they do, Maxim?"

"They made their bitches spin even harder. Russia was suddenly poisoning people, military-grade nerve agents, little green men, rigged presidential elections, hacking on an industrial scale – you name it, they said it, just like NATO told them to." Dmitry allows himself a chuckle as he recognises the various allegations. "Out they came, from their burrows. The collaborators. Online and into the media. All with the same warmongering script. Russia bad, NATO good. Only this time, we were there, watching and waiting. That's how we found the priest."

"And the lawyer?"

"NATO interrogators call it a daisy chain. See, we are using their techniques against them. The first person names the next, and on it goes, up the chain, right to the top." Maxim gives a bloody smile. "Fire with fire, but for peace."

"And the woman? Back at the lawyer's flat, you mentioned a woman: a professional?"

"The idea was to use her for all of them."

"But?"

"She stuck her nose in."

"So, you?"

Maxim nods. Dmitry crosses his arms. "Well, she is of little concern to us. But, the death of a Russian citizen, that is another matter entirely."

"To save thousands. They need to be stopped. First Iraq, now Russia, and next time? China, the Pacific rim? It could be anywhere. They're literally manufacturing war."

There is a long pause as Dmitry studies the bleeding man in front of him. "So, the million-dollar question Maxim: the daisy chain: what is the next name?"

"I was interrupted. By the ones who brought you."

"You mean you have nothing?"

"I wasn't there when he died, and I didn't find anything in his house when I went back. If anyone knows, it would be them. The woman with the stick."

Clemmie throws her empty cup at the laptop screen. "Oh great! You idiot."

Dmitry smiles to himself as he takes his first written note. Maxim's speech is faster now, and at a higher pitch. "But we know it goes to the top. We've seen the distribution patterns online. Originating from Moscow. Riga has someone on the inside."

Another note by Dmitry. Maxim senses that he is making progress.

"And your Swarm, it has a location?"

"The dark web."

"And a leader?"

Maxim gathers himself up as if speaking a sacred name: "Ksenia."

Dmitry can't hide his surprise. "A Russian?"

"And the beauty of it; she's right under their noses, in Riga. Can you imagine? Right there, in their midst."

Clemmie turns to Stig, but he is already heading for the computer. "On it. How many Ksenias in Riga?"

Dmitry's voice is more conspiratorial now. "And you have seen her, this Ksenia?"

Maxim nods eagerly. Tima produces a facial composite flip book and places it on the table. He removes the cuff from just one of Maxim's hands.

"Create her for us."

Louise scrolls through the video until she spots Maxim holding up his completed identikit. The woman he was speaking with online.

"You are sure of that likeness?"

"It's her."

Dmitry holds up the image for the camera to see, then places it back on the table.

"Don't you see what I'm bringing you? Everything. The power of the Swarm to use for yourselves. To stop NATO. To stop war."

"If we just forgive you for murdering our priest?"

"This is a war to stop war. He was collateral damage."

Dmitry sets aside his pen and paper.

"Is there anything else you want to tell us, Maxim, to help us to make our decision?"

"It's all on my computer at work. The dark web-portal, everything."

Dmitry gives a nod to Tima, who immediately leaves the room.

Clemmie pauses the video. "Shit."

She looks across to Stig who is shaking his head. "That was last night. They'll already have cleared it out."

"Still, go. Now. That can wait."

Stig reaches for his coat and leaves as Clemmie gestures for Louise to resume the video.

Dmitry brings his hands together as if preparing to draw matters to a close. "Thank you. For your honesty." They sit in silence. The longer the pause, the more Maxim's sense of anticipation grows. He tries to catch Dmitry's eye line, but the Russian just stares at his hands, deep in thought. Deliberating. Finally, he looks up at the journalist with an abrupt decisiveness. "We will give you citizenship, yes. As of this moment."

Maxim slumps, almost crying with relief. "Thank you, thank you, I knew you would understand."

"You chose Russia, and you can have Russia."

"Yes, that is what I want."

"Including our justice."

"Wha…?"

"No immunity."

Maxim's jaw drops. Blood drips down his trembling chin. "But, I thought…?"

"What? That we are barbarians?" Dmitry laughs as he gets to his feet. "Then you are very much mistaken. You will fly tomorrow."

With that, Dmitry leaves the room without looking back. The video continues to record, but the audio has been muted. Maxim's screaming cannot be heard.

*

Clemmie closes the laptop and turns to face Louise. "Thoughts?"

"Well, we've got a possible renegade NATO cell hellbent on starting a war, a do-gooder Swarm with a taste for murder, and we're in a race with the Russians to find Ksenia, not least for the sake of this person Sokolova who could be anywhere. So, all in all, just another normal day working for you."

Clemmie pats Louise on the back as she gets to her feet. "That's the spirit. Now, more tea?"

Chapter Nineteen

Stig is shown into the small glass-walled office by one of the newspaper's interns. The two-tone polo shirt and matching lanyard, which he surreptitiously secured on his way up to the editorial floor, identify him clearly as one of the company's roving IT specialists. The uniform seems incongruous with the dress sense favoured by the rest of the left-field staff. The intern, on the other hand, is evidently born for this employer; her ill-fitting pullover, bunched greasy hair and pastel eyeshadow are entirely in keeping with the general fashion consensus. Stig surmises that she will likely be offered a job at the end of her work experience, as much for her cultural fit as for any burgeoning professional talents she may have. Her voice is effervescent, but with an estuary edge. As paradoxical as her wardrobe.

"Has he got a virus or something?"

"He's not in today?"

"His laptop. You're the second person from IT who's come up."

"Ah, yes, we sent Alex last night. Big guy, short hair?"

"Yeah, the Polish guy."

Stig's smile gives nothing away. "That's right."

"But he took it down to your floor?"

"I'm here for the...desktop now. Thank you...?"

"Suzie."

"Thank you, Suzie. I'll need ten minutes."

"Right-o."

Only when Stig is alone does he shake his head in frustration. "Bloody Russians." He sets about searching the office, in a relaxed manner so as to not draw attention from anyone passing the transparent walls. There is nothing of interest, aside from the usual detritus. He then jogs the computer's mouse and the screen springs into life. No password. He clicks through the various files and emails but finds nothing noteworthy.

"Thought you could do with one of these?" Suzie, at the door, brandishing a mug of tea.

"You're telepathic, thank you."

"Any luck? Found what's wrong?"

"Just a malware that needed quarantining."

"Fascinating." She rolls her eyes and makes a beeline for the door. "Gotta go."

"Just one thing."

She spins theatrically at the threshold as if having been caught red-handed. "Yes, but no geek-speak, okay?"

"To avoid this happening again?"

"Yeeesss?"

"Did he, I mean, does Maxim keep a backup, do you know? On the laptop we've got downstairs?"

"That's not allowed."

"Of course."

"You make the rules."

"We do. And important they are too. Just would've been handy if he'd been a bad boy on this occasion, that's all."

Her laugh is a true estuary. Laden with innuendo. A glimpse of the true family behind the adopted fashion. "More bad boys, chance would be a fine thing."

He gives her a wink as he sips at his tea. "You're on the wrong floor, that's all."

Another cackle. "Oh really? I may take you up on that sometime. Meantime, you'll have to make do with the WIFI backups to entertain yourself."

Stig follows her eye line to the small white box in the corridor, between the various offices. He mimes that he is heartbroken as she spins on her heel and skips off, with the laughter still bubbling out of her.

*

Stig exits the building with the WIFI hard drive tucked under his arm and strides in the direction of the station.

Chapter Twenty

With the drive now connected to her computer, Louise sets about expanding and exploring the files. In a matter of moments, she has established Maxim's particular MSISDN number, as well as the other digital fingerprints that the in-house IT department had allocated to his accounts. She taps away, deeper into the available tracking data. "We're not going to be able to retrieve what he said," she talks to herself as much as to the others, "but we will be able to establish where he said it. Here we go. Bugger."

"Problem?"

"The dark web."

"We've lost him?"

"No. Even in the dark, you leave a trace. It's just gonna take a few hours to recalibrate what we're searching for."

Stig and Clemmie share a confused, but impressed look as Louise loses herself to her work. Clemmie beckons him into the neighbouring room. "I'm going to leave Louise on Ksenia, okay?"

"Of course. I wouldn't know where to start."

"And we've got to assume she's the route to

Sokolova."

"If I agree, can I stop all the pointless searching?"

"Yes."

"Then, yes."

"So, we just have to wait."

"Okay. And I should do that in the pub, right?"

"Nice try."

"Just don't say more cleaning!"

"I want you to go back to the church."

"For what? Lev's already told me everything he knows."

"We're going to need the help of some Russians. It's either the priests or the embassy staff, your call."

"I'll get my cassock."

*

Clemmie watches over Louise's shoulder as she narrows the search. The younger woman is now using a particular piece of software that allows her to draw a boundary box over a map to reveal all the communications emanating from within the specified area. From these, Louise can then piggyback the signal and connect to all the interconnected social media accounts that have been installed on each individual mobile device within the area. "You can literally see everything. Their entire social media presence, across all platforms."

"But I didn't think we had access to the service

computers from here?"

"We don't. It's commercially available software. Nothing special."

Clemmie shakes her head at the means and the end. "Of course it is. I've never felt my age more than right now, just so you know."

Louise gestures Clemmie into the chair beside her. "Here. Ksenia's here, see." She gestures to one of the many thousands of icons overlaid on a map of Riga.

"We used to call that a *talc*. We'd draw on sheets of acetate and put them over a map, just like this."

Louise returns the shake of the head at Clemmie's age and lack of skills. "Right. Only now, when we click on her, we can see everything she's posting and who's engaging. Media outlets in Riga, politicians in Brussels: united by their dislike of NATO."

"The Swarm that Maxim mentioned?"

"Seems to be. All amplifying Ksenia's content, in direct opposition to Riga's."

"You've already established her location? What are we waiting for?"

"Ah, now that's where it gets interesting. It shows that she's in Riga, look, I can draw a box over her location. But if I bring it up on Google Earth..." Louise opens a new window to reveal a satellite image of a lake within remote parkland. "Unless she's a fish, she's using a proxy."

"So, she's not under NATO's nose after all?"

Louise clicks through to a new overlay which shows a dotted line leading from Riga, on its way to another, as yet unspecified, location.

"Definitely not. But the source signal's encrypted. You may as well go home, this is gonna be an all-nighter."

"I can stay and make tea?"

"Go. Honestly. I'll call you if there's anything urgent."

*

The cathedral is empty and silent as Stig enters. He walks around, unsure of how to behave or what to do with himself, then finally decides to head over to the small wooden kiosk by the door, which on this occasion is also empty. He rifles through his pockets and finds a coin, which he deposits in the donation slot, then takes a candle and walks over to one of the freestanding candle-stands. A few other candles are already dotted around the metal frame, lit several hours ago judging by their diminished size. Self-consciously, he lights his candle and positions it within one of the sconces. He then closes his eyes and tries his best to offer a prayer. This is clearly a new experience for him, and he reopens his eyes and shuffles awkwardly on the spot before trying again. This time his face relaxes, and he manages a few silent words. He continues to stand like this, motionless, until all of a sudden his jaw slackens, his mouth opens slightly, and he leans his head back as if communing with an intangible force directly above him. Several minutes later, when he finally reopens his eyes, he jumps back in shock. Lev is standing directly in front of him, smiling.

"I'm going to give you the benefit of the doubt: that you aren't here in a professional capacity this time?"

Stig tries to speak but can only smile back vacantly.

"You heard him?"

Stig is evidently too embarrassed to answer the question directly. He squirms. "A light perhaps?"

Stig manages a nod. Lev seems satisfied with this answer. He steps alongside Stig and turns to also face the burning candle. "Well, let's give thanks together, shall we?"

Lev closes his eyes. Stig follows suit.

*

Clemmie arrives at the bankside just as the sun is setting. The Canada geese arc across the sky ahead of her, on their way to their evening roosts amid a cacophony of screeched conversations. She prepares for the evening. First, a coin for the lake, then the all-important ten minutes to watch the water's surface. For swirls. For bubbles. For a wealth of other subtle clues. But, as ever, The Temple refuses to give up its secrets so easily. It stares back at her, defiantly unblinking.

She strings her two rods and selects her baits. A pop-up boilie that will sit just above the lakebed silt. The small sphere is made from a mix of tiger nut meals, peanut flour and whey proteins, topped with a vanilla scent. On the other hook, a single kernel of sweetcorn on a rig that will drop deep into the sticky sediment. A hidden morsel in case The Temple leviathans are too canny for the more conspicuous boilie. She casts and attaches bobbins to her lines: small cylinders that will rise or fall to indicate any movement of the monofilament in the event of a bite. Then, she takes her seat, pours herself a coffee, and settles back to watch the sunset and consider the case.

*

Stig helps Lev as he cleans, then refills, the baptismal font. Rather than the freestanding metal bowl associated with children, this is on an altogether different scale for full-immersion adult baptisms. Somewhere between a large jacuzzi and a small swimming pool, it fills an entire room at the back of the cathedral.

"Feels like it needs a diving board."

"By this age there's usually a lot of sin to wash away."

"You plunge them in here and that's it, they're converted?"

"No. But once you're baptised you can be chrismated."

"I see what you did there, 'You.'" Embarrassed, Lev gets back to his cleaning. "Chris-what?"

"Chrismated. Chrism: another name for myrrh. It's applied to your…to the convert's forehead. To symbolise the laying on of hands by the Apostles."

"And then you're Orthodox?"

"Then you are ready to take part in the Eucharist. At that point, yes, you would become an Orthodox Christian."

"Interesting."

Lev sets aside his scrubbing brush. "Take your chance. What other questions do you have?"

"Okay, from the start, I don't get it."

"Orthodoxy?"

"What makes it different?"

The two men sit opposite each other across the room. The sound of the font's running water fills the interior with a quiet otherworldliness, set aside from the surrounding city.

"For me, it's a recognition that the Holy Spirit is here." He touches his chest. "In us. It directs us, if we allow it to."

"But doesn't everyone believe that? I mean, all believers?"

"It's more an internal relationship in Orthodoxy. Don't be fooled by all the icons. It's only through your sighs and tears that you learn to understand God."

"Sighs and tears? You're not exactly selling it to me."

"I'm not trying to."

Stig sighs heavily, unconsciously.

"There! Now that was a proper Orthodox sigh. Full of existential angst."

Their laughter rings around the small room and spills into the cathedral.

*

The bobbin twitches so subtly that Clemmie isn't sure whether it moved, was a trick of the light, or the result of tired eyes. She holds her breath, motionless, as her full attention is directed at the small plastic cylinder attached to her line. There again, another twitch. More definite this time. One of The Temple's spirits has awoken, intrigued by her offering, considering its worthiness. She reaches for her stick, ready to stand, but the bobbin stays motionless. She exhales slow and long. A false alarm. Just another momentary suggestion, an absence that proves a presence, like dark matter. Somewhere, hidden and unwilling. Just like Stig's mythical artistic life. Just like Ksenia. Quicksilver identities. Invitations to parties that the host then refuses to attend.

Clemmie turns her attention back to the main body of water. The reflected sky is now a midnight blue several hours ahead of the clock: vignetting into black at its edges. And just then, in this slate-stillness, the bobbin shoots up, hard against the rod. The reel's gears whirr into life and line tears from the spool in pursuit of an invisible force. Clemmie struggles for her stick and jams herself up to her feet. She grabs at the rod and raises the tip up high. A second or two of uncertainty, her heart in her mouth, feeling like an eternity, waiting for the line to tighten to confirm that the hook has been set. There it is. The furious thudding of a beast shaking its head, trying to loosen the metal. She again raises the rod high, at a more obtuse angle this time, to drive the hook home. This prompts an equal and opposite surge of force as the fish arcs away, around the perimeter of the darkening water, in search of the safety of reeds or overhanging branches. Clemmie holds on with all her strength as the rod pulses with indignation. A mass of muscle ranged against her, pulling at her, determining whether her resolve is equal to its own. Her shoulder spasms with pain: the deep-felt ache of an unhealed wound rekindled. An excruciating rift through her shoulder and down her arm. Fibres strained to breaking. A sensation of tearing. But she holds on, rationalising the pain as the necessary price: the sweat that now courses down her back as the ebbing away of her impurities, leaving an undiluted determination.

The fish stays deep. If the line were to break now, there would still be no evidence of this furious spirit's existence. It still does not exist beyond Clemmie's imagination. Finally, there is a flash of golden brown as the turning carp reveals its underside before careering off on another run to the far side of the lake. Clemmie's reaction is unconscious: an immediate rush of fear and adrenalin at the sheer scale of the creature she has stirred from the silt. Armoured by scales, unwilling to entertain her intent, the fish dives again with a sudden jerking pull on the line that jolts at her raw shoulder as if with expert precision. Clemmie lets out a small bark of pain, clenches her teeth and uses the chair as a makeshift support to steady herself. For over twenty minutes they wrestle. Each gaining and losing the advantage. Each trying new ways to outflank the other, both by force and by guile. And then, suddenly, as if by a switch, the great carp surfaces and lies motionless, like a vast inclusion within the lake's glassy surface. Clemmie stares at the shape in disbelief. The bronze-clad entity within the liquid silver. Mustering the last of her strength, she slowly grinds the reel's handle, pulling the sparkling silhouette closer to her in small increments. She can feel the blisters on her hands. A sharper temporal pain to accompany the deep ache within her shoulder. Closer it glides. Its heft is unthinkable. She clutches for the net and drives its gaping mesh mouth down and under the exhausted combatant. And then the resistance abates. Silence.

*

Stig and Lev sit side-by-side, still waiting for the baptismal font to refill.

"What if I wanted to convert?"

"To Orthodoxy?"

"No, veganism! Of course, to Orthodoxy."

"No."

"No? What 'no'?"

"You wouldn't be ready yet."

Stig looks less than impressed at this news. "But what just happened? What I just felt in the church."

"It's a cathedral."

The point is made. Lev rests a hand on Stig's shoulder to ensure no offence is taken. "The icons. The smells. The colours. They're all novelties to you. Like a secret society. Those are the wrong reasons."

"You said 'yet'?"

"When did you last actually read the Bible, Stig?" Another direct hit. Stig concedes with a shrug. "You must start at the beginning. Then, if God leads you to here," Lev gestures to the font, "I will be waiting."

Stig gets to his feet. Lev speaks to the water: "Look at it as a process of undoing, rather than doing. You have a long journey ahead of you. Tread carefully, my friend."

The priest doesn't look back as Stig leaves behind him.

*

Clemmie leans back and stares into the deep sky, at the faint clouds of nebulous gas and dust that find form between the constellations, an all-enveloping glory that refuses to accept the bridle of human scale. She feels her body afresh. The last of the pain leaves her, replaced now by a fluid warmth that courses through her, flooding her capillaries. She can feel the unification of her body, no longer old and damaged, but flushed through, washed clean, returned to a younger incarnation. She dabs at her eye to wipe away the sweat, but with no success. Only now does she realise she is crying. First, as single tears, then gradually more freely, until her shoulders also start to shake. She cries for the magisterial spirit that sits patiently in her net, awaiting its fate. She cries for her privilege in its capture. But also, for the past. For her weakness that the fish has revealed. For the torture she suffered at the hands of the Reaper a year before. For the physical legacy she must carry. For the choices she has made, culminating in this flawed version of herself. For that poor young boy Anatoly who died because of her in Russia all those years ago. And finally, she cries to anoint this momentary sense of liberation. The breaking away of her stifling shell, with all its responsibilities and conformities. She cries as her raw self, at The Temple's altar.

*

Old John finds her while doing his nightly rounds.

She is sitting at the water's edge, still holding the net in the water in front of her. She doesn't look up at the sound of his approaching footsteps through the wet grass. He quietly peers into her net. "Oh, Dear Lord, what have you done?" She is too tired and cold to offer anything more than a weak smile. "You've got yourself a clunker there, old girl. A scaly Temple monster." Again, nothing more than a glazed smile back from Clemmie. "Let's get you inside, shall we? You'll do yourself no good sitting here all wet." He gently prises the net's handle from her cold fingers. "I'll let her go, shall I? Would that be alright with you?" The fish's immense shoulders ease forward, as if the creature can sense its imminent release. Old John carefully lowers the edge of the net. There will be no look back from the creature in thanks for the reprieve. No acknowledgement of it having ever been cowed. Only a lesson learnt, so no other angler will be blessed with its capture for many months to come.

They watch in silence as the fish parts the lake's surface into moonlit bough waves, then dives and is lost. The blackness returns. Old John offers Clemmie his hand. "Oh, it's a mysterious place alright, The Temple."

Chapter Twenty-One

Stig and Clemmie enter the flat together, to find Louise asleep in front of her laptop. Stig heads off to make coffee as Clemmie takes a seat by the younger woman and gently shakes her awake. "Morning." Louise wipes away her dreams. "You need a few minutes?"

"No, I'm here, all good."

"We don't choose this job for the hours, I guess?"

Louise does her best to smile as she stretches. "It's fine."

"Was it worth the effort?"

"Let's see." She clicks her laptop back into life. "Well, there's a surprise!" The dotted line from Riga has completed its journey, via several more proxy rebroadcasting sites, to its actual source location: due east, in Moscow.

Clemmie leans in, incredulous. "It was them all along? The Russians?"

Stig brings coffee. "You sure that's the end of the trail?"

Louise gestures to the various icons on her screen. "She's using proxy sites to bounce the signal all over the place, but that's the source alright." She drinks deeply from her cup, then fixes Clemmie with a concerned look. "You okay?"

"Fine."

"You look awful."

"Well thank you. Long night too. So, ideas?"

Louise gets up to revive herself for the day ahead. Stig takes her seat to examine the screen in more detail. "It doesn't make sense."

"I told you, it's the source."

"I mean the motivation. If it's the Russians, why bother with the killings?"

"A warning to others, like the Skripals?"

"That's different, they were working for us. Fair game. But these others; the priest, the lawyer: why bother? And they wouldn't use a wet worker, surely? With all the OpSec risks? They'd just use their own people. Say they were visiting cathedral spires or whatever."

Clemmie adopts the opposite position to Stig's as a matter of course, to explore their thinking from all angles. "They didn't want their fingerprints on it."

Stig remains unconvinced. "You saw their debrief with Maxim. They'd never heard about all this before."

"Not those two particular men in the room, granted. Louise?"

She re-joins them, now more fully awake and

engaged. "In Russia, but not working for the Russians? There's no reason the Swarm couldn't have its base there." A collective scratching of heads before Louise pipes up again. "Or…?"

"Go on."

"Or, if the Russian Services had worked out that they were up against a breakaway cell, running out of Riga, then the Swarm could be their own covert response?"

Stig exhales theatrically. "What? Play that again."

"Well, this entire thing could be a proxy information war, without either side knowing anything about it, officially. NATO, or the Kremlin."

Stig struggles to keep up and opts for more coffee instead. "You've lost me."

Louise gestures for a refill too. "After an hour's sleep, I think I may just be hallucinating to be honest."

Clemmie paces, cogs whirring. "No, you may have something there. A forest of mirrors."

Louise is more surprised than anyone to hear this. "Really?"

Clemmie opts to sketch her thinking on a nearby scrap of paper. "If you knew that a group, maybe some alt-right nutters, or similar, were working, unofficially, from within NATO, what would you do?"

"Take them down, obviously. Before they start a war."

"So, you'd lobby NATO to clean out its own stable?"

"Yes."

"No. Because you'd be letting them off the hook. At the moment they're entirely in the dark, and in the wrong, and you want to keep it that way."

"Okay, so you'd take action yourself, but discreetly."

Stig nods too, though unconvincingly. "Right."

"In which case, the Swarm is only one of two things: genuinely a group of leftie do-gooders that the Russian services are aware of but allowing to operate from Moscow."

"Because the Swarm's doing their dirty work for them, even if unwittingly. So why intervene?"

"Exactly. Or the Swarm is the Russian Service's retaliation: a duplicate of the renegade NATO cell…"

Louise pushes Stig out of her seat as she interrupts: "Playing them at their own game. Entirely deniable."

Now on his feet, Stig comes over to examine Clemmie's illustration. He circles one of the interconnecting boxes she has drawn. "Okay, let's assume one of those is right. But then, just as the Russian Services think they have this as they want it…"

Clemmie interrupts: "NATO in the wrong and the Swarm killing any collaborators they can find."

"Yup, but then they hear from the Swarm that there may be a mole, right at the heart of things, right in the Kremlin."

"Ouchski."

"That's right. Vlad won't be happy. So, what do they do?"

Clemmie uses the sketch to order her thoughts: "Well, they can't tell the Kremlin what's going on."

Louise picks up the baton: "Because anyone could be the collaborator. Classic Kim Philby, but in reverse."

Clemmie nods. "So they'd have to continue to run things, keeping a watching brief, in the hope that the Swarm got lucky with a name." Stig smiles as Clemmie now reaches the same conclusion. "A name! It's what Liepins was trying to tell us. He thought we were there to protect him, and the rest of them, all the way to the top."

"Certainly narrows the search, doesn't it? How many Sokolovas work in the Kremlin?"

Stig rushes for his computer, but Louise stops him as she gestures to her own screen: the digital line leading to Moscow. "But hang on. Are we saying that the Russian Services are doing this outside of the Kremlin's knowledge or control?"

Stig tries to pass. "Yes, because to go through official channels would alert the mole, or collaborator, or whatever we're calling them."

Clemmie continues to add to her sketch. "Who we think could be Sokolova."

Louise continues: "Right, Sokolova. But the Embassy, here in London, doesn't know about all this, right? Nothing about their services' involvement, back in Moscow?"

"Right."

"Yes."

"They just know the name Ksenia, from Maxim, as the head of the Swarm, and now they'll be digging into his laptop. They'll think they've discovered gold, and it's only a matter of time until they'll also trace the signal back to here." She zooms in to reveal the exact source of the signal: a building: *Bol'shaya Sadovaya*.

Again, Stig tries to pass to get to his desk. "So what's your point?" But Louise hasn't finished.

"My point is that once they've got the name and the location for the Swarm, what will they do next? The one thing they are bound to do?"

Clemmie looks up from her sketch as the implications dawn on her. "They'll brief the Kremlin on what they've found."

To Louise's satisfaction, Stig now stops trying to pass. Instead, he just stares at her as he sorts the pieces into place in his mind. "Which is the worst thing that could happen."

Louise crosses her arms proudly as she surveys the others' concerned faces. "Because they'll be telling the mole everything they need to know to close the Swarm down."

Clemmie completes her sketch: "Literally, Ksenia's name and address."

Stig gestures to the Moscow address on Louise's computer. "And not in Riga, but right on their doorstep."

Louise sits back triumphantly. "No Ksenia, no Swarm, no problem."

Clemmie is already on her feet. "Unless we get to her first."

Chapter Twenty-Two

The team's false passports and visas are checked by various immigration officers without raising suspicions and they are soon on their way to Moscow. On arrival at Domodedovo airport, in line with Clemmie's instructions, Stig and Louise ignore the phalanx of awaiting taxi touts at arrivals and regroup at the building's main entrance. Clemmie then barters with these more laid-back cabbies on their behalf, and they are soon following a stocky man with short dark hair and looks chiselled in the Caucasus, to his beaten-up old Mercedes.

"We'd have paid twice as much for a taxi inside. First rule of Russia: always negotiate."

Louise and Stig get into the back of the car. Clemmie takes her seat up front, by the driver. She doesn't bother translating their conversation throughout the duration of the hour-long drive into the centre, so Stig takes his chance to get some sleep. Louise watches the changing landscape as they head up the straight main road that leads from the airport to the city. The worst of the spring snow has receded, leaving a grey slush that coats the entire landscape.

Mile upon mile of dense woodland, specifically firs and silver birch trees, line their route as the driver bobs and weaves his way through the heavy traffic. When dwellings do finally come into view, they are arranged in definite bands: first the traditional wooden dachas on the outskirts; then, the vast grids of Soviet apartment blocks; next, the more aesthetically pleasing architecture of the old city; and finally, the impersonal glass and metal skyscrapers of the centre. And all the way, at regular intervals, large billboards scream for attention, promoting everything from cars and bank accounts to music concerts by bands that Louise vaguely remembers from a decade before in the UK.

By the time they arrive at their hotel, the city is already dark. Peking Hotel is located in the heart of the old city and stands as one of the remaining monuments to Stalinist classicism. Despite the current owner's best attempts to modernise the interior and bring it up to date for the many travelling businessmen who seem to constitute the majority of its guests, the rooms still evoke a Soviet austerity that no amount of garish wallpaper can hide. Cheap, functional, brown chipboard combines with dripping taps and flickering lights to imbue the place with a uniquely retro sense of menace.

Once they have unpacked and freshened up, they meet downstairs and head out into the bitter night. It is a picture of icy grey, interrupted only by the stream of car taillights that course ceaselessly through the night. Clemmie evidently knows the area like the back of her hand from her time stationed in the capital. She does her best to show them the immediate area, including the most appropriate escape routes back to the airport in case of trouble. At the end of the tour, she guides them to the Starlite Diner on *Strastnoy Boulevard* for a much-needed bite to eat. An exact copy of a 1950s American diner, Starlite cuts a surreal silhouette in the raw bleakness of the night. With authentic red-leather bench seats, laminated tabletops, stainless-steel ribbed edging and a small-town US menu, it provides a burst of garish colour within the all-pervading grey slush. They are met by a spotty Russian teenager, dressed in period costume, and shown to one of the alcoves. Louise surveys the interior with evident disdain: "How very Russian."

Clemmie hands her the menu. "It's popular with Westerners. So, for the time being, we won't be overheard by the locals. Milkshake?"

Stig takes a moment to observe the other diners, as much out of interest as for professional counter-surveillance purposes. Clemmie is right; the plastic tables are indeed populated by a range of loud Americans and other English-speaking nationals. These over-sized foreigners make no attempt to speak Russian to the waitresses, or to each other. This is evidently a home-from-home venue, with the portions as inflated as the clientele's sense of their own superiority. Stig feels suitably ashamed.

"We will eat, sleep a few hours, then head out when there are fewer witnesses, agreed?"

The others nod. Over Clemmie's shoulder, Stig sees a pair of young girls enter the restaurant and scan the room with the strangely glazed expression adopted by internet dates the world over: a fixed serene smile to avoid revealing disappointment should their blind date fail to live up to their profile photo. A fat Rolexed hand beckons them over and they are soon sitting across from two much older Americans who give them a drooling welcome. It is clear the girls have never met these men before, despite the over-friendly public charade being performed for the benefit of the rest of Starlite's diners. Prostitutes, Stig surmises as he returns his attention to Clemmie, who is outlining the night's mission on the back of a serviette: "I will take a position at the exterior of the building here," she says. "Stig, you will cover this arc, here, at the top of the stairwell. Louise, you gain access to her flat, here."

"Through the front door?"

"It's on the fourth floor, unless you want to fast-rope in through the windows?"

"Understood."

"When she answers the door, you move up to

provide cover, here," she says to Stig. "Press the entrance buzzer twice to notify me that you're inside, and I'll come up to join you. Are we all clear?" The others signal their agreement as they select their food. "Good. We will approach on foot; it's a short walk from our hotel."

Louise hands the menu to Stig. "And what's the objective? Assuming she's in?"

"We get her out of there with the minimum of noise and fall back to the hotel. We can debrief her there."

"And if she refuses?"

"We persuade her. Whatever it takes."

They fall silent as the waitress reappears to take their order. Stig uses the distraction to refocus on the two old Americans. The two young girls are now sitting between them on the bench seat. The proximity only increases the age discrepancy. The girls are barely pubescent, the men in their late fifties, by Stig's estimation. Only partially hidden by the half-eaten waffles that litter their table, the Americans' meaty hands are soon all over the girls: kneading their pale young thighs just below the line of their short skirts. The waitress has gone. Stig notices that Clemmie is staring at him. She follows his line of sight.

"Do we have a problem?"

"Just getting aquatinted with the local customs."

One of the old Americans notices he is being watched. He momentarily removes his hand from the girl, but then changes his mind. With a smile of unapologetic power, he stares back at Clemmie and Stig as he drives his hand hard up, under the girl's skirt, causing her to wince with the pain. Stig starts, but Clemmie places her hand on his arm with a whisper: "Not our business."

Stig settles, to the evident delight of the American, who continues to manhandle the girl. Clemmie clicks her fingers to draw Stig's attention back to the table. "Now show us what you've got."

Stig retrieves his laptop from his bag and opens it, facing away from the rest of the customers. "On the flight, I checked the Kremlin's employment records."

"There was a match?"

"Anna Sokolova. Personal assistant to the Public Affairs Officer, a Gleb Abakumov."

"Responsible for?"

"Creating mass public support for the Kremlin's policies, including defence."

Louise scrolls through Stig's file, including Sokolova's photo and her employment record. Thirties. Petite. Redhead. Her hair and makeup are finished with a confident restraint that is neither under nor overstated. The overall effect is one of varnished competence: reliability and efficacy personified.

"She has access to every strategic communications brief and helps to draft every policy statement. With just a few keystrokes, she can shape the entire public debate."

Clemmie nods her respect to Stig, but also to Riga for the scalp. "You've got to hand it to them: the NATO team. She's perfectly placed."

Stig gestures to Clemmie's serviette-plan: "You still want to go for Ksenia first?"

Clemmie nods as she pours water over the serviette and scrunches it into a ball of inky pulp. "Yes. Our priority is to keep her alive. Find out what she knows." She surveys the image of Sokolova. "This one: her time will come."

Chapter Twenty-Three

They leave the hotel individually, managing to avoid catching the eye of the burly overnight receptionist who is anyway engrossed in the late-night Channel One News. The anchors are discussing alleged airspace violations, by Russia, over the Baltics. From the snippets of the programme's audio that Clemmie can hear as she passes the front desk, they make a good fist of sounding exasperated, before pivoting to the build-up of NATO military jets in Romania.

They meet up on the corner of *Brestskaya Ulitsa* and follow the *Garden Ring* road, by foot, south-west for a hundred metres, before dashing across the busy thoroughfare and then returning north-east on the opposite side until they come to the building: *Bol'shaya Sadovaya*. It's a grand new build, neighbouring the *Aquarium Garden*, with five floors of apartments above a ground floor of trendy technology companies and marketing agencies. The facade is dotted with balconies, seemingly one for each apartment, and small, double-glazed windows within the mustard-coloured plaster render. A utilitarian austerity as much for the bitter weather as for any architectural vision.

A small restaurant to the left of the main entrance, long closed for the night, provides the ideal nook in which Clemmie can stand and observe the street without drawing attention to herself. Meanwhile, Stig and Louise make light work of the exterior door locking mechanism and are soon inside and climbing the stairs. On reaching the fourth floor, Stig holds his position at the top of the stairwell as Louise makes her way down the stark hallway to the correct flat. A few moments later, in the freezing cold, the entrance buzzer to the block of flats rings twice and Clemmie is granted access.

*

Clemmie enters to find Ksenia sitting at her glass dining room table, sipping at an espresso. She is elegantly dressed, with a minimalist classic style in keeping with the interior decoration. The overall impression is of modern, restrained wealth, as distinct from the garish opulence of the previous generation of Russians whom Clemmie used to know. Clemmie pauses to survey the surprising state of affairs. She glances at Stig and Louise but only receives embarrassed shrugs in return.

"I let them in." Her English is precise, albeit with a strong Russian accent.

"You were expecting us?"

"I always expect someone." Only now does Clemmie see the MSS pistol on the table beside her.

"Coffee?"

Clemmie shakes her head and takes a seat opposite her hostess. Stig and Louise remain standing, instinctively covering the exits. Clemmie finishes her scan of the room as Ksenia pours herself another shot from an elegant stove-top pot. The mass of technology and wires have been carefully hidden by the interior designer, but they are there, humming in the background. Ksenia notices the focus of her attention. "Welcome to the Swarm. That is why you are here." A statement, not a question.

"Yes."

"Your accents. English?"

"Yes."

The two women survey each other. Ksenia: tight-faced, powdered white, long black hair, red lips: unchanged from her appearance on Maxim's video conference and his identikit depiction of her for Dmitry. A carefully crafted vampish caricature. Clemmie: lined with time and pain. A faded elegance beneath a greying bob.

"And you are?"

"A vested interest. A friend. We are here to warn you. Protect you, even." Ksenia raises her eyebrows as she glances at her pistol, then at Clemmie's lack of a weapon. "The Kremlin knows about you, which means the collaborator knows about you."

"You come well briefed." She drains the last of her coffee and places the cup down with utmost care. Delicate fingers: in a previous Russia they would have been perfectly suited to a musical instrument rather than a computer keyboard. "But I'm not currently recruiting for security. Thank you for the offer though."

"The pistol. An MSS?"

"So?"

"The *Vul*. 'wool' in English. Manufactured specifically for assassinations by the KGB. And still the go to for many within the FSB and MVD."

"Is that what you think is happening here? That I am, that we are...?" Ksenia trails off as she laughs at the suggestion. She stares at the three of them in turn. "You could not be further from the truth."

"So, you are vigilantes then?"

"We are, an antidote."

"Administered on whose authority?"

"The people's."

"And do you think the people would agree to you murdering in their name?"

"I thought you were here to warn me, not judge me." Clemmie acknowledges the point with a nod. "You are spooks, yes." Again, a statement, not a question. "From where I'm sitting that makes you part of the problem, not the solution. Spooks, soldiers, politicians. On both sides. You are the ones taking us to war."

"It's not that simple."

"Really? Well, we think it is. And we are seizing the power back from people like you because you've misused and abused it. Everything that you have been doing in our names, and what you haven't been doing. Just sitting there watching as a war is conjured from nothing. Why, because it suits you? Or because when Russians die, they don't count? It's very simple. We are the antidote to your actions, and your inactions."

Clemmie speaks with a quiet deadpan clarity. "The services here know about you, but haven't stopped you. Why? Because you are doing their dirty work. You're a part of the very apparatus that you say you're against."

Ksenia laughs away the suggestion. "Of course we know. We're exposing NATO for the warmongers that they are, and they'll want to give us medals here for that. But when we find the name of the collaborator, we'll bring down half the Kremlin as well. Those who knew, those who should have known and those who were paid NATO silver to turn a blind eye. Then they'll cease to love us so much."

"If you work with us, we can—"

Ksenia interrupts Clemmie with a wave of her hand towards the door. "I need your protection as much as I need your permission: not at all. Now, thank you for your visit, but please leave. I have work to do."

Stig catches Clemmie's eye, as if asking for permission to make his move, but she shakes her head fractionally. She turns back to face Ksenia with a deep sigh. "The collaborator in the Kremlin. I know the name."

Ksenia's demeanour changes instantly: "What dd you say?"

"The daisy chain. The lawyer. Liepins. He whispered it to me before he died."

"You?" Ksenia inspects Clemmie through narrowed eyes, then calmly picks up the pistol, cocks it and aims it at her head. "Then you know what I will do to get it."

Louise inches closer but Clemmie gestures her back. She leans forward, slowly, across the table, until her forehead is resting on the muzzle of Ksenia's pistol. "You will only get one shot off." She gestures to Louise and Stig on either side of her. "And then they'll kill you and they'll have to complete this mission without either of us. Do you think they will manage? To successfully avert war. Just the two of them. Or d'you think they'd prefer to have us around to give them a hand?" Ksenia examines Louise and Stig, and clearly isn't impressed. Clemmie continues: "Now, I personally think they can do it, but what about you? Pull that trigger if you believe in them. If you'd like the vested interests that you say they represent to see this through on your behalf."

Ksenia slowly removes the pistol from Clemmie's forehead and places it in her lap. "So, what is your price? For the name?"

"We also need to identify who's running this. Not just here, but in Riga. We're on the same side. Come with us."

Ksenia laughs. "Just like that?"

"Just like that. You were about to shoot me, and I'm still offering you protection. I think you can trust me."

Ksenia gestures to the enclosed computer wiring that encircles them. "This. I can't just walk away, with the flick of a switch. The entire Swarm. It will take hours to power down."

"We have as long as it takes. Then tomorrow, to London. Until it's safe."

"For the name."

"So you can finish what you started." Clemmie nods towards Stig and Louise. "They can stay with you here tonight. While you do what you need to."

Ksenia looks at them again, almost embarrassed on their behalf. "No thank you." Stig and Louise seethe but stay quiet. Clemmie gives them a sympathetic glance as Ksenia continues: "The collaborator will know what we have done to the others. They will be focusing on their own survival at this moment. We have time."

"So, we have a deal?"

"When the time comes, we get to deal with the collaborator our way. The Russian way."

"As you wish. With a smile, like the priest?"

Ksenia laughs lightly at the thought. "We are on a crusade for peace, so we take our inspiration from the Bible. The smile: he died as the 'holy fool'."

"And the lawyer: a needle, wasn't it?"

"'With the venom of crawling things of the dust.' Deuteronomy."

"How poetic."

"This is Russia. I don't need to tell you of all people how cruel it can be." Ksenia checks her watch. "In five hours, I will be ready."

Clemmie leans on her stick and raises herself from her seat. "Then, until the morning."

With that, they leave the flat.

Chapter Twenty-Four

The Peking Hotel's dining room is a white, marble-clad affair with cold service to match the food and decor. Prostitutes who have finished servicing their clients in the rooms above now sit in the corner, comparing notes. Clemmie and Louise drink coffee while Stig awaits his food order. He is the first to break the silence. "The ethics of this. Protecting Ksenia so she can whack Sokolova: aren't we here to try and stop all the killing?"

Clemmie waits for Stig's congealed spaghetti to be served. Louise stares at it with revulsion. The waitress leaves. Stig gets stuck in but looks back up to Clemmie for an explanation.

"If we leave Ksenia in play, then Sokolova will have her killed, sooner or later. So, either way, one of them is going to die. Out of the two, Sokolova is preferable."

Stig speaks as he eats: "Why?"

"Because her death is more likely to halt the escalation in the region."

"And the ethics?"

"It's the morally sound choice, given the options."

"But not ethical?"

Clemmie glares at him. "It's moral because we are trying to get the best result from a wholly shit situation. Ethical? Well, we only have two choices, Stig. Unless you have a better idea?" He withdraws to his spaghetti. "Why are we even having this conversation? This is the job. If you want to feel better about it, go talk to a priest."

They return to silence, with none of them particularly happy with the result of their brief exchange. Louise tries to break the tension: "Isn't that..?" She is looking across to the huddle of prostitutes: one of the girls from the Starlite, now with raw red bruising around her face and neck. No doubt a parting gift from the oafish American. The other prostitutes briefly sympathise as they examine the damage, then continue with their previous conversations. This is evidently not an unusual occurrence.

When he speaks, Stig's tone is snide and directed at Clemmie: "Well apparently we just ignore it. Just the way it is. It's a cruel city, like Ksenia said. Christ, I can't wait to get out of here. What time's our flight?"

He looks up for Clemmie's answer, but she is just staring at him, wide-eyed.

"What is it?"

"That's right."

"Wha…what's right?"

"'I don't need to tell you of all people how cruel it can be.' She said that. Ksenia."

"So? It's a shithole? I totally agree."

"But how would she know?"

"Er, look around!"

Louise is now interested. "How did she know that you'd been here before?"

Stig remains unconvinced: "It was a turn of phrase, so what?"

Clemmie shakes her head. "'You of all people.' That's not generic, that's specific."

Louise has a moment of inspiration. "She is FSB or MVD, despite what she says? The pistol? They'd have files on you from back then?"

To her annoyance, Stig doesn't share her excitement. "We're talking decades since Clemmie was last here." He checks that no offence has been taken before continuing, "They wouldn't keep backups from so long ago on the main governmental systems. No way."

Clemmie nods her agreement: "Stig's right. You'd have to know the files were there in the first place. Even then, it would take days, weeks even to dig them up. And anyway, we're here under false names."

"And we never introduced ourselves."

"She couldn't have got them from here."

They shift in their seats and fidget as they each try

to rearrange the cognitive chess pieces. Louise winces as she speaks: "No, it couldn't be."

Stig is on her wavelength. "Riga? But how, that can't be, it would mean…"

Back to Louise. "She is communicating with the people she is in the process of taking down?" She turns to face Clemmie, who is just staring into the middle distance with a glazed look. "Clem?"

Clemmie finally turns, but still unfocused. "They are directing her. Oh my God, that's brilliant. They're controlling every aspect of this." The others frustratedly gesture for her to explain. When she speaks again, it is with a new reverie in her voice. "It's a masterpiece. The secret unit within NATO. The collaborator in the Kremlin. And the Swarm clearing up after them. They're controlling the stimulus and the response. Both sides. They whole game."

Stig puts down his fork reluctantly. "You've lost me."

"They create the conspiracy: that there are collaborators. Next, they control Russia's response. Then, they pour fuel on the flames from within NATO. On and on. And they use the Swarm to kill everyone that has had anything to do with them along the way. Covering their tracks, permanently, as they go." She shifts in and out of intelligibility as she marvels at the complex beauty of the strategy. "How could I have not…? Who could have…? This is genius."

Louise tries to coax her back to the here and now. "So you're saying is that Ksenia is one of them? We're clear about that?"

Clemmie now focuses: "She has to be."

"But we don't know who they are?"

"No."

"Only that the Swarm is theirs."

"Not originally. But now under their control, yes."

"And the renegade unit in NATO?"

"Yes. But them, from the start."

Louise and Stig exchange an utterly confused look. He picks up where she left off. "But, if she's one of them, how come she doesn't know about Sokolova, who is also one of them?"

"Oh, she doesn't know she's working for them. That's the brilliance. She still believes she's independent. You saw that yourselves."

"And Sokolova?"

"Oh, she'll definitely know she's one of them. But not that Ksenia is."

"Any why?"

"Because then she'd know that she was going to be killed in the end. They'll have given her assurances of course. But empty promises."

Stig slumps back heavily into his chair, unable to make sense of anything his boss is telling him. He looks to Louise for help but gets none back. "I have no idea what you just said, what you meant, or what we are supposed to do now."

"Now, well, we have to go. Obviously."

"Obviously?"

"Well, if they told her about me, then they must know we're here. Don't you see?"

This new information jolts Louise and Stig into a sudden state of high alertness. Stig scans the room around him with a renewed sense of concern, then leans in to speak more discreetly: "What did you say?"

"They must do. Why else would they have told her? And she was expecting us."

"And we have no idea who these people are?" He checks over his shoulder. "They could literally be anyone."

"But we know where they'll be."

"Do we?"

"Of course. Keep up. C'mon." Clemmie throws down enough money to cover the bill and leads the way to the exit.

Chapter Twenty-Five

They approach the building using a new route; again on foot, but from the east, through a maze of backstreets. They arrive at the rear entrance as dawn is breaking. The mustard exterior seems to glow of its own accord. Stig whispers: "How do you want to play it?"

"Louise, with me, in case there's trouble." Stig is clearly a little affronted, but Clemmie doesn't give way. "She spent last year in the gym, you didn't. You, stay here. Watch our tails. Call if anyone follows us, okay?"

"Fine."

Clemmie leads the way. Louise turns to Stig and inflates her cheeks, then follows. Stig takes a position under a nearby silver birch tree and grumbles to himself. Louise catches up with her boss. "Trouble? What kind of trouble?"

*

Clemmie ascends slowly to the fourth floor, as much because of her stick as any wariness. Louise keeps a floor's distance between them, then holds back at the top of the stairwell as Clemmie eases along the corridor towards the door to Ksenia's flat.

It is slightly ajar. Clemmie pushes it fully open with her stick. She gestures for Louise to join her. The younger woman leads the way inside in silence.

The ransacking is immediately evident, despite the minimalist decor. The glass table has been shattered and now exists as a carpet of sparkling confetti under their feet as they steal through the interior. The few ornaments and items of furniture have been similarly smashed and scattered. Ripped wires are all that remain of the flat's inbuilt computer system.

The two women inch forward, listening intensely for any sounds of movement, but the interior is eerily silent. Louise edges to the cusp of the main room, in which they met Ksenia earlier that morning. She spots the dark pool of blood on the polished concrete floor before she sees the body. A few steps further and Ksenia is fully revealed, still in the same elegant clothes, but otherwise unrecognisable. Her face has been appallingly disfigured by the force-feeding that ultimately killed her. Her jaw sags down, broken to accommodate the handfuls of food that have been so violently stuffed into her mouth and through the back of her neck. Louise just manages to stop herself from being sick. "What the fuck is that about?"

Clemmie looks over the grim scene with calm disdain. "You know your Bible?"

"Not this bit!"

"'For I was hungry, and you gave me food. I was

thirsty and you gave me drink, I was a stranger and you welcomed me.' Ksenia, from the Greek. It means 'stranger'."

"Religious, so it looks like the Swarm." Louise looks away from the body determinedly as she speaks. "So this was, or wasn't, Sokolova?"

"No."

"But I thought you said she was…?"

"The top of the daisy chain? She is. But they won't even tell her. Because if they do, she'll know she's next. Once they've finished with her."

"So, we go try and save her instead."

"No."

Louise shrugs imploringly. "Okay, help me here! Like, why would they do this? You said that they wanted her to kill Sokolova for them?"

"Our arrival. We spooked them. No pun intended."

"But how could they know she was going to work with us? We only just spoke to her."

"They didn't. But our arrival, like everything else: they're using it to their advantage."

"How do you mean?"

"You can imagine the article in tomorrow's papers: 'NATO collaborator visited by British Secret Service'…"

"Of course, your file."

"Collaborator and agents murdered by vengeful

Russia. Further proof of NATO warmongering and some extrajudicial killing of agents to add plenty more fuel to the fire."

"Jesus, this is…"

"Brilliant? Yes. We've been played from the moment we landed. And if we don't leave now, we'll be the ones to take the rap for this."

"And the agents bit?"

"The what?"

"You said, the 'collaborator and agents murdered': that's us, is it?"

"Let's just make our flight, shall we?" She gestures Louise back towards the entrance. "And then all we've got to do is work out who's doing this, and how to stop them before they start a third world war."

"Right. Excellent."

*

Clemmie and Louise peer down at Stig from one of the small, fourth floor corridor windows as Clemmie simultaneously calls his mobile. They watch him answer. "Is everything alright?"

"Act natural."

"Okay, so what's going on?"

"Make it look like you're chatting to a friend." She waits until Stig starts his performance on the street below; as if he is having a free-flowing chat on his mobile. "We're too late. She's dead."

Stig doesn't react visibly, but his voice adopts a nonchalant sing-song quality. "Oh that's great news. How wonderful."

"And we may be next."

He maintains his big smile. "Well that's also outstanding. Really outstanding. And any more good news from your side?"

"Now Stig, look around you. It's likely they'll be waiting for us. Does anyone have eyes on you? We can't see from this angle."

Still burbling to his imaginary friend, he checks in all directions. "No, I'm really sorry mate, I can't see you on that day. Any other suggestions you've got?"

"Check again. Be sure."

Another look, but this time there is a slight hesitation. "Ah, absolutely, I can see you then my man. Just you, is it? And you'll pick me up in your wheels like usual?"

Clemmie covers the mouthpiece to swear, before returning to the call. "I'm hearing you. So, that's one up. Male. In a car, yes?"

"Spot on. Really looking forward to it."

"Okay, stay nice and relaxed, that's it. Now listen carefully…"

Chapter Twenty-Six

Stig, still talking on his mobile, walks briskly along the pavement, back in the general direction of the Peking Hotel. He searches for a one-way street and walks in the opposite direction to the flow of traffic. Unable to follow him by car, the lone driver gets out and picks up his tail on foot. Stig turns sharply into the *Aquarium Garden* and uses the change of direction to look back and catch a glimpse of his disciple. Overweight, pale skin, likely from smoking, and a receding hairline. Stig increases his pace with a new spring in his step.

Styled in the pre-revolutionary era as a set of kitchen gardens, this small oasis of water fountains and arches seems ill-at-ease with the incessant bustle of the surrounding city, but it is ideal for Stig's purposes. He increases his pace yet further, to a jog, as he passes a sculpture of Satyr, the wood nymph, playing his pan pipes to a row of empty benches. On any other occasion, Stig would have enjoyed the intimate beauty of the gardens, a celebration of cultural romanticism, but not today. Instead, he heads quickly to the park's rear corner and vaults the wrought-iron fence, confident in the knowledge that his middle-aged pursuer will be unable to follow. He then runs full pelt past the *Mossovet* theatre and out towards the main road, only glancing back to enjoy his wheezing shadow's frustration behind him. Within moments, Stig is lost among the early morning hubbub. He calmly waves down a passing car and offers enough money to get the driver's attention. "Airport. Domodedovo. Yes?"

A few more notes, and Stig is soon on his way.

*

Using their mobiles to choreograph their movements, Louise and Clemmie exit the building in opposite directions, but at exactly the same time.

"Talk to me."

"I'm clear."

"Are you sure? Check again."

"I'm sure."

"Right, you know what to do."

"But what about you?"

"Just stick to the plan."

"Right-o. Laters."

Louise rings off. Clemmie surveys the street in both directions. The single male figure makes no attempt to hide himself.

*

Louise returns to the Peking Hotel and clears their three rooms. She bundles everything into a single suitcase, sits on it to make it close, then heads down to the front desk to settle up. A different receptionist is now on duty, no longer the burly lump from the previous night. This is a smart, clean-shaven young man with excellent English and perfect nails. As she waits for the bill, Louise catches sight of the small TV behind reception that remains tuned to Channel One. Although she cannot understand the presenters, it is clear they are discussing the relative strengths and weaknesses of the various military vehicles that have been deployed to the nation's southwestern border.

"Your car will be here in just a few moments. Plenty of time until your flight, madam."

*

Clemmie does her best to keep changing direction in an attempt to lose her disciple, but to no avail. He is all over her; a competent professional. In younger years, she knows she would have made light work of him, but not now, at her age and in her current condition. She has no chance. Finally, without further options, she chooses a public location, beside a street kiosk selling every imaginable type of cigarette, then simply stops and turns to face him. Even from this distance, she can see his thin smile as he realises she is choosing to confront him, rather than continue with her fruitless attempts to escape. Maintaining eye contact, he approaches her slowly but confidently. He is the predator, and they both know it.

He is in his forties, heavy-set, with a long dark coat in which he keeps his hands hidden. He could be carrying; she cannot be sure from this distance. His confident gait and unsettling physicality suggest he has seen action, perhaps in one of the breakaway states. But this isn't someone who spent the twelve months of their conscripted national service just seeing out time. This is a man with a significant degree of training and a self-assurance that only comes from time and experience. This is someone who joined up because they wanted to be in uniform and stayed because they enjoyed their work.

As he comes to within just a few feet of her, he slows his pace. She can feel the scan of his eyes. First, for the likely location of a concealed weapon. Then, for the possible weight and range of her stick. Rather than play this game, she opens her jacket slightly to reveal her waistband and under her arms: no weapon, no threat. His continued smile is one of mutual respect between two professionals. He appreciates her hopeless courtesy. As he closes in on her, Clemmie can see that there is indeed something in his pocket. There is a movement under the heavy cloth as he changes his grip on the item. A new tautness in his shoulder, as if clutching. This is no syringe or pistol. Rather, the physical preparation suggests brute strength. A knife, or an ASP, perhaps. With his final approach comes the slight loss of focus in his eyes. A look she recognises all too well. The momentary, involuntary, blurring of the vision: an evolutionary trick to avoid being haunted by the violence of one's own actions. She closes her own eyes and braces. She exhales and makes peace with the cold darkness. On the lakeside now. Resigned to forces beyond her control. And there it is, the sound of a fast approach, the rush of wind close to her…but not as expected. No surge of pain with the impact. Instead, a new noise: screeching. A wheel on the kerbside. She snaps her eyes back open and just catches a glimpse of his heavy jacket flaring behind him as he runs. The soles of his shoes, receding. Then, a second figure, giving chase, now slowing to a walk, and finally to a stop. Turning. A recognisable face. Dmitry. Her own breathing coming back under control as he returns to her. A kindly smile. "You, okay?"

"Yes. Fine. Thank…"

A gesture towards his black car, parked at an unholy angle on the kerb beside her.

"Get in."

*

Their drive to the airport is considerably smoother than her journey into the city the previous day. The graduated architectural styles in reverse, giving way to the thick forest. A dark green anaesthetic to numb the unpleasantries of the past twenty-four hours. "These are the workers' dachas; not so expensive because of the main road."

"Yes."

"But still good enough soil to grow cucumbers. Everyone should pickle. Do you pickle?"

"No, that's not something we do in England."

"You should. Everyone should pickle."

"Who was he?"

"We don't know yet. We'll find him though. On one of the hotel cameras."

"So, not Russian?"

Dmitry tries his most charming smile, but still manages to look vaguely menacing. "We are not your enemy."

"And Ksenia? That wasn't you either?"

"No. The same man. He waited."

"You were watching everything?"

"Yes. Since you arrived in Russia."

"But you chose not to intervene?"

"Everyone is fighting each other, but not us. It's like watching sport."

Clemmie leans her forehead against the cool glass of the window. The roadside trees are closely packed together, creating an impenetrable barrier, even for light. A dark world behind a green veneer, on the other side of the window. A riddle wrapped in a mystery.

"So, what next?"

"I drive you to your colleagues, at the airport. Then you fly home."

"You know what I meant."

"That depends on you. You know the name. We don't."

"If you're thinking of torturing me for it." She gestures to her stick in the backseat. "Don't bother. I won't crack."

He laughs, but only half-heartedly. "We have changed since you were last here. I am sorry for what happened to Anatoly, and to you, of course."

His intent is good: sympathising for the death of her former agent. They had tortured him with an electric drill. The same technique as used on her a year ago, albeit by different hands. But Clemmie doesn't welcome the comment. Her eyes narrow. "You've read my file?"

"Of course. I'm sorry, I didn't mean to upset you."

"How did you get it? When?"

He can see her disproportionate concern. "At the Embassy in London. Did you think we wouldn't search you? Your visit was of immediate interest to us."

"You, or Nikolai? Who asked for it, specifically?"

"Well Nikolai, of course. But we retrieved it. Myself, with Tima. I don't see the significance. What did you expect? Are you okay?"

Deep in thought, she waves him away. "I asked, what next?"

Dmitry can still feel the tension emanating from her, but carries on regardless. "If you give us the name, we will take care of the situation here: Russian soil, Russian business."

"And what do we get, in return?"

"In addition to saving your life?"

Clemmie settles deeper into her seat. "You owed me that. For Anatoly."

"Whoever they are, they have people here in Moscow, off our radar. Just like in London. We are both blind. By working together, we can give each other the gift of sight."

"A miracle indeed."

"Or we can continue as enemies and risk war."

"Feels like blackmail, not a choice."

"We offer our friendship, Clemency, as an ally. We can use this to build the relationship between our countries. Nikolai is very clear about that."

"Is he now?"

"That has to be a good thing, no?" From his short glances as he drives, Dmitry can see that she remains unconvinced. "You know, he insisted that Maxim's interrogation wasn't shared with official channels; with the Kremlin."

Without looking, he can sense that Clemmie's

interest has been piqued. She is now sitting back up straight in her chair. "Nikolai? And why would he do that?"

"To watch."

"To watch what?"

"If anything happened, then it couldn't be because of the collaborator. It could only have been triggered by your arrival."

"He used us as the bait."

"You came here without telling us, under false names. We didn't use you. We just…"

"Used it to your advantage."

"Exactly."

Again, Dmitry can sense, but not fully understand, her concern. "Why does that make you angry? He briefed us to protect you, not her."

"Nikolai? And why would he do that?"

"Isn't it obvious? He needs you. Russia does. We can't convince NATO that they are being played, just like we are, because they'll never believe us. And we can't appeal to your boss, the illustrious Chief, because he is rather predisposed to thinking the worse about us 'Ruskies', if you hadn't noticed." She smiles her recognition. "We don't have the name, or a way of getting it. Well, without resorting to torture of course." He checks to see if this gets another smile. It does. "Nikolai genuinely believes that the only way to solve this is if you want to tell us the name, yourself, of your own free will. Of you seeing the sense of us working together. He's a progressive. And thank God for that."

They drive in silence for a while as Clemmie considers the facts.

"What will you do to them, if I give you the name?"

"To start with, nothing. Why would we remove the baton just as the conductor is about to play their symphony? Whoever is doing this, they are making fools of us. All of us, yes? We aren't too proud to learn from their greatness."

"And then?"

"When the music finishes, the show is over. Well, then the curtain must come down."

His meaning is not lost on her.

*

Dmitry's car is waved through the airport's barriers and he draws up right outside the main entrance. The taxi touts fade away behind their clouds of cigarette smoke, like retreating squid. He steps out and moves around to open Clemmie's door. He gives her his hand to help her to her feet and then retrieves her stick from the backseat.

"Thank you."

"I was told to make sure you got your flight."

"For earlier. For what you did."

189

He gives an embarrassed smile. "We look after our friends. It is the Russian way."

There is a long pause before Clemmie speaks: "Sokolova."

He isn't surprised by the name. She watches him process the information, making sense of its immediate implications. He then gives her a nod of professional respect, just as she had done to her attacker just a few hours before. "Thank you. For your trust."

He offers his hand. They shake.

"You suspected her?"

"No. But it makes sense. Her access. Her responsibilities."

"And you will leave her in play?"

"Until the end of the performance. You have our word." He walks back round to the driver's side. "Have a safe flight, my friend."

Clemmie watches his car pull away.

Chapter Twenty-Seven

Clemmie finds the other two sitting by the departure gate, waiting for it to open. Stig stands and offers her his seat. "Here, please."

"No, I'm fine. Stay where you are."

"Please, take it, I can't stand looking at him any longer."

Clemmie follows his line of sight to one of the other gates, on the opposite side of the corridor. The two loud Americans from the Starlite diner are there, awaiting their flight out of Moscow and using the time to letch over every female airport employee naive enough to enter their orbit. "Well, at least he's leaving."

Clemmie accepts the seat. Louise offers her the rest of her coffee. "Any problems?"

"No, all good. No issues."

Louise senses that Clemmie is hiding something but respects her wish not to talk. "I got your stuff from the room by the way."

"Thank you."

"And we're not delayed at least."

They run out of small talk and end up just staring

at the departures board and the nearby TV, which, like every other set in the country, is tuned to Channel One. Anything to ignore the Americans. Clemmie finally breaks the silence: "This has been an unmitigated disaster, hasn't it?"

Stig perches on the back of Louise's chair so as to speak quietly: "What will you tell the Chief?"

"Jesus, I don't know. Russian soil, Russian business, I guess."

"Nice line."

"Dmitry just said it to me."

The other two double-take. "Dmitry?"

"As in Embassy-Maxim Dmitry?"

"Don't ask, okay? It won't help, not now. I'll tell you on the flight."

Louise and Stig share an affronted glance but keep quiet. They return their attention to the TV. Out of the corner of his eye, Stig sees the handsy American announcing to his friend that he needs a "piss" and heading off to the nearby toilets. Stig checks that Clemmie and Louise are still absorbed by Channel One's wall-to-wall coverage of the escalating tension on the Russian border, then follows. "Back in a sec."

*

Mid-stream at the urinal, the paunchy American squats slightly to fart, then zips up and heads over to wash his hands. He doesn't immediately recognise the other man staring back at him, via the wall mirror, from the neighbouring basin. It is only when he is shaking his hands of the excess water that the dawning realisation registers on his face. It is soon replaced by a look of twitching concern. "Now son, let's not get all fired up over some commie hooker, you hear me?"

The American steps backwards, taking him beyond the range of the mirror's reflection. Sounds of violence fill the room.

*

Clemmie speaks under her breath: "Well, that didn't take long."

Louise is also focused on the screen. "That's Maxim, isn't it?"

There, sitting alongside a diminutive but perfectly turned-out young woman in her late thirties, is a tired Maxim, reading a statement to the camera as part of an official press conference. A band of text scrolls across the bottom of the screen, which Clemmie translates: "Anna Sokolova, Assistant to the Director of Public Affairs." It is Sokolova's briefing; Maxim is merely there as her prop. He performs the function of the repentant sinner while she watches over him like an elegant confessor. He pledges allegiance to his new nation, then tells the audience his colourful story: of wayward priests, crooked lawyers and the hidden hand of NATO.

The audio is so faint as to be barely audible above the unrelenting tumult of the airport interior, but the thrust of the narrative is self-evident on account of the short animations that illustrate Maxim's tale. The locations and methods of the various murders, intercut with footage of NATO's recent military exercises in the region. On finishing his monologue, Maxim is then escorted from the room by a brutish young man in an ill-fitting suit and Sokolova takes her place in front of the assembled media to answer the battery of follow-up questions.

Stig reappears from the toilets, holding a paper hand towel across his knuckles as if he is still drying them. "What's going on? Can you hear what's being said? What're they doing? Is that…?"

"Sokolova. Yes."

Her face gives little away as she talks, whether as a result of Botox, or a practised professionalism. An image of Ksenia appears picture-in-picture as she explains with calm authority the consequences of NATO having stooped so low as to kill extrajudicially on Russian soil. This act transgresses all accepted international humanitarian standards, and Russia is therefore, left with no choice but to defend itself against such brazen aggression. Clemmie stares into Sokolova's television eyes. "Retaliating against their own provocation. A war with themselves: controlling every piece on the board. The start of their endgame."

Louise joins Clemmie. "Who the hell is doing this?"

Stig gestures to the window, in the general direction of Moscow, beyond the forest. "We should go back. We've got to stop her."

Clemmie shakes her head slowly. "No, not her. They're running this remotely."

"Who then? We can't not do something."

Clemmie allows herself a smile as she studies Stig. "That sounded a lot like a presumption to save, eh Stig? A bit of saviour complex after all?" He looks bashfully at his feet. "Good. That's the spirit." She suddenly spins on her heel and marches off down the corridor, seemingly unhindered by her stick. "C'mon."

"Hang on… Where are you going?"

Clemmie calls back over her shoulder: "Riga!"

Louise chases after Clemmie. Stig stands gesturing meekly to the departure gate, which has already started accepting the first of the passengers onto the London flight. "But…?"

Finally, he throws the paper towel into a nearby bin and runs to catch up. The American's blood is lost among the rubbish.

Chapter Twenty-Eight

Father Lev is in the process of dressing when his mobile rings. "Hello?" His smile is immediate on hearing the other voice. "Ah, hello, and how are you?"

He becomes suddenly more serious as he listens. He rushes for a pen and paper. "Yes, go on."

*

The taxi pulls up outside the Holy Trinity Orthodox Church at a little after midnight. The car's headlights reveal the deep-red terracotta of the building's heavy perimeter walls, but the rest of the church, including its confection of domed spires, remains silhouetted against the moonlight. The muddy low-tide smell of the nearby Daugava hangs like a thick mist in the night air. They pay their driver and wait in the still blackness. Moments later, a side doorway opens and a cassocked man descends a short staircase into the car park. He is slight, mid-thirties and with a beard that sparkles golden-white within the light from the single candle he holds for illumination. "You are?"

"Bryan, yes, hello." Stig offers his hand, but it is ignored by the priest.

"I am Father Michael." Stig blanches at the mention of the name. "Yes, Father Lev said that this would please you. The archangel. Your prayers have been answered. Now, shall we?"

Louise rolls her eyes but chooses to say nothing as Father Michael gestures them into the church's dark interior.

*

"It's basic and cold, but God is with you in all that you endure."

Clemmie looks around the bare stone room and tries her best to appear grateful. "It's perfect, thank you."

"And discreet. Father Lev said that was the priority?"

"It is."

"Well, I will let you get some rest. We celebrate Matins at an hour before dawn. You are very welcome to join us."

"Thank you, but…"

Stig interrupts: "I will. Yes. Thank you."

With a slight nod to Stig, Father Michael leaves the room. Louise and Clemmie try their best not to exchange a smirk, but Stig can feel the change in the atmosphere. "What?"

"Nothing."

"We need their help, right?"

"Absolutely. Get to know them. God drills, I

mean, good drills."

The women snigger as Stig retrieves three camp beds from the shadows and begins arranging them. He positions one very far away from the others.

"Ah, you don't want to associate with us sinners any longer?"

"I don't want to wake you up, if you must know!"

Clemmie tries to introduce some maturity into proceedings: "Thank you. That's appreciated."

Louise surveys Stig's chosen location, near the door. His bed happens to be right under a wall-mounted crucifix. "I've heard of being closer to God, but that's ridiculous."

Stig fires her a look, and they all get on with unpacking their things and laying the tattered blankets over their beds. Unable to resist, Louise holds one of the worn pieces of material up to the moonlight coming in through the ceiling-height window: "I guess that's what they call a holey blanket, is it?"

Stig tries to ignore the sniggering from the darkness on the other side of the room: "Oh yeah, very good. Have some respect at least."

"Sorry, you're right."

Again, several moments of silence pass before Louise's voice can be heard once again, whispering this time: "Hey Clem, what does God call his nose?"

"What?"

"God *knows*!"

Stig just tucks himself under his blanket as the other two try, unsuccessfully, to stifle their laughter. "Nighty-night."

"Yeah. Night, mate. Hey, one thing though. Stig?"

"What is it?"

"How does Moses make tea?"

"Go to sleep."

"No seriously, how does he do it?"

Stig sits up, less than impressed. "Go on."

"He brews. Get it, Hebrews it."

Louise has to bite her arm to stop herself laughing. Finally, even Stig smirks before hiding himself under his blanket once again. "Hell-arious."

*

There are just six other worshippers in addition to Stig: all clergy. Father Michael is leading the service, although also facing the iconostasis, with his back to the others. His slow, quiet chanting is in Church Slavonic, so unintelligible to Stig, who simply lets the sound wash over him along with the thick swirls of incense. He leans back occasionally to look up into the vast dome that rises to darkness above them. Despite the language barrier, he makes a point of taking part in the service as best he can. He follows the example of the men around him and crosses himself on multiple occasions: three fingers pressed together – the index, middle and thumb – first to the forehead, then to the waist, then the right shoulder, then across to the left. Repeated. Once the service is complete, he is ushered in silence into an adjoining room and seated in front of a bowl of buckwheat at a worn wooden table. No accompaniments, just buckwheat and a glass of tea. He eats in silence, as do the others on the bench beside him.

*

Stig is already sitting back on his camp bed by the door, deep in thought, when Clemmie awakes. He returns her smile but remains silent as she stretches, struggles to her feet and inspects the interior, now with the benefit of a slash of daylight from the small windows above. The room is no less forbidding by day. Entirely functional, it contains; three camp beds, a simple wooden writing table and chair, and nothing else, aside from the wall crucifix. As gently as she can, Clemmie pokes Louise awake with her walking stick. Louise, also without a word, nods an acknowledgement to the others and gets herself ready for the day ahead. The laughter of the following evening has gone. Maintaining their silence, like an unspoken agreement, they exit.

*

The British Ambassador's residence is a spacious open-plan affair, with mellow wooden floorboards, an array of uncomfortably formal sofas and myriad paintings on every wall. The artworks are all by contemporary British painters and chosen by the Ambassador from the Foreign Office catalogue that rests on the coffee table for the perusal of awaiting guests.

Stig and Louise sit side-by-side on one of the sofas in awkward silence. Clemmie remains standing by the grand piano in the far corner of the room, opposite the entrance. At one point, the three visitors are joined by two elegant cats that enter, survey the ensemble, then leave again with disdainful flicks of their tails.

When the Ambassador does finally arrive, it is on a bow wave of assistants who brief him from their smartphones, then dissipate into other areas of the building. He is of medium build, with grey-brown hair topping a flushed drinker's face. He wears a blue suit, blue shirt, blue tie and immaculately polished shoes: as unimaginatively dressed as all British ambassadors the world over. With exaggerated deference and a hot fleshy handshake, he introduces himself and, having unsuccessfully offered tea to the others, pours himself a cup from the already-cold pot with noticeably shaky hands. Finally, he sits back in the only visibly comfortable armchair and dunks a biscuit. "Rich Tea. There are still some things we do so much better than the rest, don't you think?"

Clemmie speaks quietly but doesn't cross the room

from the piano. "Ambassador, we apologise for the short notice, but if I tell you the reason for our——"

His interruption has an unapologetically dismissive tone: "I have been briefed on the way up."

"Good, then you will understand our need to gain access?"

"You can't just go wandering around the compound. No matter who you are. Once were. On whose authority at any rate?"

"On yours, Ambassador, we were hoping."

"The name's Mark. And no."

"Mark, this is a matter of the highest priority——"

Again, the interruption is clipped and intentional: "And with whom do you want to parley? That's not even clear to me."

"The head."

"Of the whole place?" He chokes at the idea and manages to lose half his biscuit in his tea in the process. "Buggeration. I take back what I said. Where do they manufacture these now, China?"

The others watch as he spends a moment trying to fish the tea-sodden fragments out of his cup with the aid of a small silver spoon, until he finally gives up, sets the tea down on the table and returns his attention to Clemmie. "No-can-do, not in this timeframe, nor indeed in this manner. International ripples, that's what it'd cause."

"Ambassador, Mark, we are talking about an escalation towards conflict."

"And I have no intention of starting one here to boot, in my own back yard. That's not how we do things in Riga. Especially not when dealing with the Centre for Excellence. You can't just go bouldering in there unannounced. Anyway, they've got a course on at the moment. Otherwise engaged."

"It wouldn't be unannounced if you—"

The speed of interruption is decreasing. "So many countries. Too easy to cause offence. No. Mild manners, and plenty of warning. That's how we do things. Exactly to avoid the conflicts."

"This is with Russia."

"Even that seems far-fetched, if I may say. At most we're talking about some local unrest. No one's seriously suggesting the Russians will go to war over this, are they?"

Clemmie controls her rising anger at the expense of her voice, which cracks noticeably: "Events may not be being determined by Russia, that's the whole point."

She knows that he knows that she has given him his get out. "And I'm quite sure that tone wouldn't go down well with our esteemed military allies."

Clemmie takes a deep breath and puts on her best smile: "Mark, I'm sure you can understand our feeling of urgency. And I can only apologise that we didn't quite have time to send a formal letter of request."

"Anyway, how would you know who you were meeting? One of the kosher lot, or one of the shifty ones you say are causing all this fuss?"

She walks over to take a seat beside him, on the nearest uncomfortable sofa. "We wouldn't. Not at first."

"Spells trouble, whichever way you order the letters."

"But at least it doesn't spell war."

He spends a moment thinking it through. "Sorry, just not the way we do things."

The sighs from the others are audible. Clemmie's mood changes. "So, you won't help us?"

"Can't, rather than won't, old girl."

Louise snorts at the description of Clemmie. With the sweetest of smiles, Clemmie now leans in close to the Ambassador: "Right, well, in that case, let me just say one last thing to you…"

*

"And don't come back!"

Clemmie, Louise and Stig are shown roughly out of the Embassy compound by two of the security team. Despite nearly succumbing to a slapstick fall, Clemmie does her best to maintain her dignity. "Sodding useless!"

Stig tries to speak, but Clemmie is in no mood to listen. "They breed them to be this incompetent, you know that?"

"He did—"

"At private schools. They have dances to marry them off to each other. Because no one else would want them!"

"He did say—"

"I own pot pants with more intelligence."

"...one thing that was useful."

Finally calming, Clemmie gestures for him to continue. "Surprise me."

"There's a course on." He speaks slowly to talk her down. "And what do courses have?"

Two pairs of eyes now focus on Louise.

"Students."

Louise is immediately suspicious. "Hang on."

"The kind of students who go to the gym."

Clemmie's smile is now as conspiratorial as Stig's. "And who know a thing or two about cyber."

"I can't just...? How?" As if to answer Louise's question, the compound gates open and a dry-cleaning van passes, joins the main road and heads northeast across the Daugava, en route to the city centre. "No."

Stig makes a note of the address on the side of the van. "Oh yes."

*

The dry cleaner is nestled at the end of a cobbled backstreet in Riga's Old Town. The old man at the counter is surprised to see the state of the blanket his customer has spread across the reception desk in need of repair. In his best broken English, he spends a few minutes trying to explain to the young man that he would be better off buying an entirely new bed covering, but the language barrier is too great, and he ultimately agrees to complete the job. With his attention so entirely consumed by Stig, he doesn't notice Louise in the shop behind him, sizing herself up against the rows of pressed military uniforms in their cellophane sleeves.

Chapter Twenty-Nine

L ouise wears a military uniform as it should be worn, with the shirt sleeves rolled up three finger-widths higher than the elbow joint, and with a bicep substantial enough to fill the fabric. Anything less represents a lack of personal discipline, both in terms of attention to detail when dressing and intensity when training. She has no trouble passing as a professional soldier within the crowd of similarly robust military personnel of all ranks who steer their way through the entrance gates and into the NATO Strategic Communications Centre of Excellence's main compound.

The perimeter security is laughably lax considering, or exactly because of, the number of soldiers in attendance. As with so many military establishments around the world, the sentries seem to have assessed that if anyone is stupid enough to either try to gain access falsely, or otherwise target such a large group of trained killers, they are likely to regret their endeavour. The holding up of a security pass is, therefore, enough for most of the soldiers, including Louise, to enter without requiring them to interrupt their earnest conversations about the many hybrid wars being fought, in secret, around the world. Only the unlucky few, on either side of the main camouflaged column, are required to have their passes inspected.

Once inside, they pass a forest of flagpoles representing all the various nationalities of students in attendance, and then move on towards the lecture theatre and the afternoon's presentation: 'Target Audience Analysis: creating and calibrating appropriate parameters'.

The theatre's raked seating is of the grey tubular metal and corresponding grey padding favoured by lecture theatres and hotels in the 1980s. The audience faces a room-length stage, complete with a permanent lectern and accompanying on-stage seating for group discussions. A metal bell is rung to signal the start of the lecture, and the audience of several hundred military men and women stand to attention as a senior member of the course's Directing Staff takes his position behind the lectern. At the second sounding of the bell, the soldiers sit and are then subjected to a two-hour lecture peppered with enough three-letter acronyms to confuse all but the most diligent among them.

The overall effect of the speaker's relentless droning, coupled with his use of such unapologetically complex language, is to coax the audience to the very edge of sleep. Heads start to drop in the darkness, only to be jolted back up by the speaker's occasional bumping of his microphone and the corresponding wail from the PA system. Louise can't help but see the entire scene as a piece of immersive satirical theatre, complete with a modern-day clown on the stage. If this is the official School of Excellence for NATO's future strategic communications operators, then it is perhaps not surprising that a renegade unit within its ranks may have taken matters into their own hands.

The rush for the coffee machine in the break is neither surprising, nor elegant; the student soldiers evidently now perceiving caffeine as an existential need rather than a mere pleasurable interlude. Louise uses this scrum as her chance to break free from the rest of the crowd. Having first surreptitiously relieved the crushingly dull Directing Staff member of his entry pass, she makes her way through various magnetic doors, away from the educational area of the compound and towards the restricted live-monitoring zone.

*

Within just a few corridors, identical in their cream industrial vinyl flooring and framed photos of the centre's alumni through the years, she is in a noticeably different style of interior. Identikit wooden laminated doors now line the corridors, with metallic plates that designate the capabilities that lie within. 'Media monitoring', 'Plans', 'Production' and 'Cyber'.

She continues her journey apace, deeper into the interior. It will not be long before the owner of the pass notices its absence. If she is between two sets of these magnetic doors at the time, she will be trapped red-handed. Until, that is, the arrival of the Military Police to release and then incarcerate her in quick succession.

The other soldiers she passes – the permanent members of the Centre's operational staff – are courteous and entirely uninterested by her presence within this restricted area of the facility. The regular rotation of faces from around the world ensures new operators are barely noticed. Like any international military environment, there is just a generalised sense of camaraderie between uniformed colleagues that supersedes any deeper connection.

She passes a series of doors that are noticeable exactly because of their lack of door nomenclature. Instead of the previous literal descriptors, the name plates now offer only ascending Roman numerals. As the door to 'IV' opens and a tired-looking man heads for the nearby toilets, she manages to catch a glimpse of the interior. Even from such a brief look, she is able to ascertain that this is a country cell. The array of computer screens and TV feeds inside are all covered with different recognisable news sources from East Africa. She is in the right place. These are the region-specific teams, comprising native speakers under the stewardship of officers from the usual NATO lead countries. She is close now, albeit having found the wrong room and with the clock against her.

*

The Russia monitoring room isn't hard to locate, as all Louise has to do is follow two stunningly beautiful soldiers – distinguishably from the region by their high cheek bones and feline eyes – back from the coffee machine to the door marked 'VI', at the far end of the corridor. Sure enough, the sound of spoken Russian can be heard as the soldiers re-join their colleagues. Louise busies herself examining someone she thinks she recognises in one of the wall-mounted cadre photos until the coast is clear. She then retrieves her mobile phone from her pocket and opens the *what3words* app. She heads to the end of the corridor, directly outside room VI, and takes a screengrab of the three words that designate her position to within three metres. Next, she heads back to the coffee machine and roots around for one of the wooden spatulas that have been provided for mixing the cream and sugar. She snaps one of the lengths of wood in half and uses the rough edge to cut a small hole in the left-hand breast pocket of her uniform. She then switches her phone onto video record, drops it into the pocket and does her best to line up the lens with the hole that she has just made. Finally, she walks back down the corridor, knocks twice on the door to VI and enters without waiting for a reply. Fourteen heads turn to face her from multiple computer screens, with a fifteenth moving quickly towards her. "Yes, hello?"

A tall officer, mid-thirties, the rank of Major. Sandy hair and quick blue eyes. He is soon standing right in front of her, blocking her view of the rest of the room.

"I'm sorry, is this not East Africa?"

"No, that's number four."

Louise gestures forlornly at the number on the door. "But I thought…?"

With a dramatically condescending tone, he raises his hand to gesture at the door to illustrate: "Four: the 'I' goes in front of the 'V'. This is six. The 'I' goes after the 'V'. Gottit?"

The act of raising his arm enables Louise to see into the room behind him. She moves her position slightly to ensure that her camera gets a clean sweep of the background. "I'm so sorry. An Oxford education, just unfortunately in a state school."

He gives a short smile as he begins to close the door on her, then stops suddenly: "Oxford, you don't say?"

Louise can feel the blood drain from her face with every word of his next sentence. "Me too. Which school were you at?"

Louise reels. Why did she need to embellish? Hadn't they told her repeatedly during training: the bigger the lie, the bigger the trap.

"Well, it was a long time ago…"

"You can't remember the name of your school? How old are you? A few years younger than me, right? Where did you go?"

She can feel his blue gaze boring into her. "Are you alright?"

"Fine. Just need to get to Africa. Late for a meeting." Louise takes a few steps back into the corridor and gestures herself towards the correct room, but the Major is evidently suspicious. He steps into the corridor after her. "The one with the I before the V. On your left now." He is watching her. She has no choice but to reach for the handle. Her slow actions make him even more suspicious. He is walking down the corridor towards her now, without hiding his look of distrust. She can hear his words as if through water as she reaches for the door handle that seems to move away from her as she stretches towards it. "What unit are you with?"

Then a second voice, behind him. "Major. Major?"

He turns, angered. "What is it?"

"You need to see this; they're moving hardware into the buffer zone."

The news supersedes his concerns about Louise.

"Are you sure?"

Louise takes her chance. She confidently opens the door to the East Africa room, enters and closes it behind her. The Major is torn. He turns back momentarily as if to speak to Louise once again, but she is already gone, so he quickly follows his team member back into their own room and the unfolding events on the Russian border. Moments later, Louise remerges from room IV with sincere apologies and the same story about her diminished schooling, although this time she omits to mention Oxford.

*

Louise exits the compound with a determined gait, as if late for something important. She only exhales as she rounds the corner of *Kalnciema lela* street, out of sight of the compound's sentries, and into view of Stig's big dopey welcoming smile.

"I've never wanted to go to church more in my life! Let's get out of here."

Chapter Thirty

To the accompaniment of chanting from the church above them, the three set about examining the video from Louise's pocket camera. She freezes the frame and creates a screengrab with each new face that is revealed. By the end of the process, they have a full set of all fifteen faces.

"The Russia cell."

"And somewhere in there is the cell within the cell. But how many and who?"

Stig surveys the photos. "And this one?"

"Major. From Oxford originally. State school educated." She sees Stig's impressed look at this level of detail. "Don't ask."

Clemmie is pointing at the *what3words* screengrab. "And this?"

Louise clicks between programmes and brings back up the software she previously used in the Tooting flat. "We can specify the exact location, here, then draw our box over it. At least one of them had their mobile phone switched on, against the rules."

"Naughty, naughty."

Louise clicks through various screens. They are

soon looking at the social media feeds belonging to one of the women at the very back of room VI.

"And the others? I'm assuming they didn't have their phones on?"

"It will take time, but I'd put money on one or two of them being connected on social media. I can do a facial recognition search against this first woman's profile, then go from there."

"A daisy chain?"

"Of a kind, yes."

"How long? Another all-nighter?"

Louise shrugs. Clemmie gives her shoulder a reassuring squeeze. "Well, there's not much else to do here, I guess? Unless you wanna go to confession?"

Louise laughs as she gets to work. "This should only take a few hours. Confession: I'd be here for days."

*

Clemmie and Stig wander around the empty church to pass the time.

"So, what is it that's hooked you?"

"How do you mean?"

"Orthodoxy. It's clearly got under your skin. If you don't mind me asking?"

He gives a big sigh. "No, not at all. But I'm not sure what I can tell you."

"So, you believe in God?"

"Yes, I think I do. I felt Him." They share a glance at the double entendre. "Don't go there."

They walk a little further, then take a seat and survey the many frescos on the ceiling and walls above them. Angels and doves. Jesus on various cloud thrones.

"Looks a lot comfier than our camp beds. So?"

"It's binary. Believe or don't believe. I like the certainty. There's a confidence in conviction. Oh, and the communion wine, of course."

Clemmie chooses to ignore his levity and studies him with genuine interest. "Is that what you've been missing? The certainty?"

"Maybe. No shades of grey."

"I envy you. Sort of."

"You could…?"

"No." Clemmie gets back to her feet, but Stig stays sitting. "You want me to leave you here alone for a bit?"

He nods. "Yes. Thank you."

He listens as her stick clicks away into the darkness. It is only after several minutes, as his eyes adjust properly, that he sees him, also sitting alone, on the other side of the nave. Father Michael. In his hand, a long black knotted rope, barely visible against his cassock, moving slowly but incessantly as the knots pass between his thumb and forefinger. They share a slight smile. Then the priest returns to his prayer, and Stig to his thoughts.

Chapter Thirty-One

The dawn chorus spills through the small, open window and echoes around the stone room as Louise's computer grinds to its conclusion. She gives the others a shake, and Clemmie and Stig are soon up and out of their beds, drinking from the carafe of cold water that constitutes the only available breakfast.

"Good morning."

"Well?"

"Success. Sort of."

Clemmie takes Louise's place on the only chair and stares into the screen. "Show me."

"There are two distinct groups. Here…" She reaches over Clemmie's shoulder and clicks between wireframe representations of the various social media connections that exist between the fifteen members of the Russian cell. "The majority: these eleven, they are connected to each other by at least one social media account. And then here, this second group of three…"

"Connected to each other, but not to the rest. What about the fifteenth?"

"The Major. He's the only one that spans both groups. Stands to reason if he's the team leader."

Stig now joins them by the screen. "But this just shows that there are different friendship networks, right? Like in any office?"

"Ah, yes, but..." Again, another few clicks and Louise has a new infographic on display. The smaller group of three, plus the Major, is now laid out in a circle. The computer begins to fill in the blanks around, and connections between, these individuals. "When I scraped for more on this lot, look what started to appear." Boxes of shared interests, like Venn diagrams, manifest between them. Their online behaviours, preferences and a wealth of other open-source data points, innocuous in isolation but revealing when aggregated.

"Cookies, registry hives, configuration files; they all paint a picture. What they've been looking at, reading, the ads that have caught their attention: thousands of tiny indicators. And, of course, who they have been targeting."

Even through Clemmie's uninitiated eyes, the similarities are glaringly evident: the most hawkish news sources; the most partisan and divisive online groups; the most inflammatory topics among the most hostile oppositional parties and commentators; the systematic monitoring and targeting of the most suitable distribution channels and the most inflammatory voices. A shared focus on that which will divide, rather than unite. Both sides of every argument. Carefully manufactured for maximum effect. NATO's stimulus and the Swarm's response.

Clemmie and Stig just watch on in wonder as Louise continues to manifest usable intelligence from this wealth of raw information. "This is the infrastructure of the whole damn thing. Every one of their collaborators, and their dissenters. Every online argument. The kindling that will burn with just the right inflammatory content. The mechanics of their entire deception."

Like constellations in the night's sky, the visual data form new lines of intersection before their eyes: previously unseen connections and meanings.

"So, we have them?"

Louise closes her laptop. "Yes. We have them."

Chapter Thirty-Two

Major Anthony Newton has a robust confidence that needs no words. The crisply pressed military uniform with its razor-sharp creases along the arms and trouser fronts, the highly polished toecaps, the precise fading of the clipped hair under the beret he removes on entering the café. This is a man entirely at home in his own skin, albeit a skin provided by his chosen profession. He orders a takeaway cappuccino with a soft intensity that leaves the barista in no doubt of his responsibility to deliver to the very best of his abilities, then positions himself at the end of the bar to await his order. He surveys the other customers with a serene smile, as much for the chance to enjoy some early morning eye candy as for any reason of professional situational awareness. There is the usual smattering of uniforms, as would be expected so close to the compound, as well as civilians with identity passes: the camp's cleaning staff most likely.

And there she is. Sitting alone at a corner table, staring directly at him. No longer in uniform, but now in jeans and a dark-blue hooded top. Louise breaks eye contact in the full knowledge that intrigue will get the better of him and he will approach. Of course, he will. She represents an unanswered question.

"Oxford?"

He is smiling down at her, takeaway in hand. In semi-silhouette, his physicality is even more pronounced. The lines of his shoulder muscles contour his uniform.

"I think we both know that bit wasn't true."

Again, the desired effect. Interest piqued. A more pronounced suspicion is etched on his face, but also an enjoyment of the chase. Louise gestures to the seat opposite her. He takes it.

"How very mysterious." A new flirtatious undertone. "So where did you grow up, if you don't mind me asking?"

"Leicester."

"And the reason to lie?"

She laughs. "Trust me, you really don't want to know."

The first glimmer of concern in the eyes. "Are you perhaps a student on the current course?"

"No. I'm not even in the military."

The concern compounded. "But you were…?"

"Wearing a uniform? In a restricted area of a military camp? Snooping around the Russia cell? I know!"

He clears his throat, reaching for the higher

ground. "I don't need to tell you that what you just said…?"

She interrupts, now icy: "You're right, you don't." She eases from her chair and takes a seat at the neighbouring table, just as Clemmie enters the café and takes the place opposite Newton. There is a flicker of recognition from the soldier, which he quickly buries. Clemmie orders coffee and waits for the waiter to leave.

"Major. Or may I call you Anthony?" He gestures his approval but remains wilfully tight-lipped, waiting for Clemmie to continue. "Of course, you know who I am. From my file…which you gave to Ksenia." He doesn't flinch. Clemmie smiles at his recalcitrance. "A little before you had her killed. And all to protect your prize asset: Sokolova."

He reaches for his phone, but Stig pushes his hand back into his pocket as he also draws up a seat. "Oh no you don't, big man."

The Major sighs as he leans back and surveys the three of them around him. Clemmie continues: "But now there's no need to skulk around in the shadows, is there? Russia has reacted, officially. And for every action, there will be an equally official reaction by NATO. On and on." She applauds him silently. "Until what? All-out war?"

Another sigh, but this time for effect. He raises himself in his chair and smiles. "You won't even get to the end of this street before I have you picked up."

"Unless we strike some kind of deal. Here and now."

A full laugh: robust and unapologetic. "You have nothing on me because there is nothing. I am simply a servant to my country, and to NATO. Reacting appropriately to events."

"It's all very well-choreographed," Clemmie interjects. "We've said as much, haven't we?" Stig and Louise nod sarcastically.

The Major refuses to be distracted from his point. "You, on the other hand," gesturing now to Louise on the next table, "illegal access to a NATO base. A dead body while you were in Moscow. What to make of it?"

"Oh, I'm sure you got it all figured out. All part of the master plan."

His smile is intentionally cruel. "More evidence of a NATO conspiracy. Fuel to the fire on an already volatile situation." He leans in. "Just by being here, you have made things unimaginably worse. Thank you." He gets up, pushing Stig away firmly in the process. Clemmie motions for him not to react. "Whatever you thought you would achieve with this theatrical nonsense, you failed. But then, if I'd seen your file like you say, maybe I'd have expected that." He enjoys the fury in her eyes as he continues: "You fail, and Russians die. It's like a pattern. Isn't that right?" He is about to leave but pauses to enjoy the moment. "Maybe, Clemency, you need to face facts. You're a washed-up old woman with a pair of part-time sidekicks." He watches her wince with his every word. "Oh sorry, did that sting a bit? Funny, despite all the lies, the truth still hurts. And now you've stepped into a hybrid world you don't even understand, let alone know how to control. And your response: a walk up over coffee. That's the best you've got? Do us all a favour and piss off back to your fishing. You survived Moscow, but next time you may not be so lucky."

He heads for the door. Clemmie's voice is quiet behind him. "And you think they won't kill you?" He turns to face her, to see if she is bluffing. "You think you'll be different: special?"

"They need me here, within NATO."

"They did. But this is official now. NATO and Russia: acting and reacting. You just became a loose end. Just like Sokolova."

"You have no idea."

"It was you who gave Ksenia my file. So now, whoever you are working for knows that you are willing to kill your own. The lowest of the low. You think they'll want to keep you around? That they can trust you?"

His smile is more forced than before. "Does this patter normally work? Did Anatoly fall for it?"

Clemmie holds his gaze, calmly and patiently. "But, the thing is, you couldn't have known about my file. A grunt like you wouldn't have access to the service's records." He refuses to take her bait. "And anyway, you're not senior enough to access it, Major." Again, not even a twitch of anger from him. "So, there must be someone on the inside, and much more senior, who is running this, and running you. Someone who recognised your overinflated sense of self and used it against you, who made you believe you were indispensable." The first involuntary twitch at the edge of his mouth. "And you swallowed it, like a good 'un, didn't you? Like the dumb, low-ranking egotist that you are." Another twitch. "Hook, line and sinker." She gestures to the chair he just vacated. "Now sit down, you vile little man. Time is against us."

*

Newton tries to maintain his charade of grandeur despite feeling Clemmie's eyes boring into him from across the table. "A name."

He summons all the defiance he can muster: "This is so much bigger than you realise."

"So, they're in government? A minister? Just give me the name."

He laughs bitterly. "You think this is just us? A colonial hangover? British influence post-Brexit? It's existential."

"What is?"

"No threat, no alliance, no funding: from the contributing nations."

Clemmie glances towards Stig and Louise, as if unable to comprehend what she just heard. "This is about money? Is that what you...? You're starting a war for NATO's budget?!"

"Not a war. Just an escalation. The politicians and the public: they need to be resensitised."

"Resensitised?"

"They need to feel the fear, so they continue to write the cheques. He spoke to them. The military commanders across NATO. They are in agreement."

"So, it is a 'he'?"

Newton nods. "When the time's right, Sokolova will withdraw, and NATO will de-escalate. There'll be no war. All according to his plan."

"This isn't a renegade conspiracy, it's NATO policy?"

"People need to be reminded of our worth. That we underpin everything. The structures they take for granted. The entire fabric that gives them freedom."

"You are out of your mind."

"Oh, don't pretend it's ever been different. Oil, trade routes, control of seaports: it's always about money. NATO must fight for its budgets like everyone else. But today's politicians refuse to pay. They want cuts without compromise. All the gain, with none of the pain. We have to re-educate them. Remind them. Force them. An effects-based operation on our own side, for their own good. Why not?"

"And Russia in all this?"

"Forget Russia. They're far less of a threat than our own politicians!"

Clemmie shakes her head, which infuriates Newton all the more. He says, "And who are you to judge? We finally have someone to fight our corner using modern methods. NATO is aligned. There will be no war. Just a better-funded peace. What's wrong with that?!" His confidence is building once again. He puffs himself up in his seat. "You'll get no name from me. He'll reveal himself when the time is right. As the man who protected NATO, so that NATO can continue to protect the world."

Clemmie takes a moment to collect her thoughts. She studies him with a mix of tenderness and pity. "This – his – entire plan is predicated on the belief that, having marched Russia to war, they will just back down when the time comes?"

"Of course they will. It's in everyone's interest to de-escalate as soon as possible. That's the beauty of it. A revenue drive based on peace, not war."

Again, she takes her time before speaking. He watches her impatiently, as if waiting to shout down any argument she is about to make.

"Thirty million."

"What?"

"Around thirty million. That's how many Russians died in the Second World War, defending the free world you claim to represent. And look what you've done with it."

"Oh, don't lecture me." He tries to get to his feet but is blocked by Stig and Louise. Unable to pass, he settles back down with a petulant sigh as Clemmie leans in closer to him. "They know about Sokolova, but they haven't lifted her, and they haven't killed her. Why?" He struggles to find a quick retort. Clemmie continues, now in a whisper: "Because they understand your game and they want you to play on. To draw you deeper and deeper, out of your depth. You think you are in control? They invented the game, you idiot. Centuries before your *hybrid*! Genghis Khan. Napoleon. The Eastern front. More recently, Syria. Because they know that in the end, they will be prepared to pay a greater price than you. For what they believe in. Not money, but something much more valuable: principles."

Exasperated, he stares at the three of them in turn. "Did they turn you into a bunch of Trots while you were in Moscow?"

"You think they will pull back because you tell Sokolova to? Seriously, you actually believe that? Now they know what you've been doing: warmongering? They'll go to war exactly *because* they understand what you've been doing! Because you need to be stopped. Because of what you've become, and what you have done with the freedom that was bought with Russian blood." His bravado is waning; he listens more carefully as Clemmie continues: "And you know what? They'd be right. And at the end of this, when God knows how many people are dead, history will remember them kindly. The Russians, not you, because they will have fought on the side of right. Whoever came up with this plan missed one vital consideration: the Russian soul." Clemmie changes her position and her tone. "Major, for all I don't know about your techniques, I do know about theirs. You are in my world now, young man, and if you want to keep us all alive, I suggest you start helping me. Give me a name."

All eyes are on him. He remains motionless for an uncomfortably long time, before finally looking up and smiling to the heavens. "The daisy chain in reverse. How very ironic." They watch him squirm as he tries to scrabble around for the last of his composure. "I want... no mention of me... that is my price." Clemmie nods her agreement.

"Finch. His name is Finch."

The others exhale, blowing the tension out and away. Clemmie gets to her feet. "Thank you."

In silence, Stig hands Clemmie her stick. Louise leads the way to the door. At the last moment,

Clemmie turns back to Newton, who remains seated at the small table. "One last thing."

"Yes?"

"You are a disgrace to that uniform. Any Russian soldier could tell you that."

They leave. Newton avoids the barista's stare from behind the bar. He pulls himself up in his chair, checks his creases and reapplies his generic officer's smile. Although, on seeing his own reflection in a nearby mirror, even he is not fooled.

Chapter Thirty-Three

The flight remains eerily smooth, as if the plane is still stationary, rather than lunging through the night's sky. With Stig and Louise asleep in nearby seats, Clemmie tries watching a film, but is too distracted to follow the story. She presses the button for the stewardess and places her order: a cup of camomile tea and a glass of crisp dry white wine. She positions them on the fold-down tray in front of her and drinks each in turn. First, the tea to calm her mind, then the wine to kindle her imagination.

She closes her eyes and lets the alcohol take effect. The watery movement of colours and patterns behind her eyelids. A glimpse of The Temple: that scaled titan, the deep-felt pain, physical and emotional, then the tears in the cold night.

The pieces of the puzzle begin to swirl through the water around her. The names on the list – all dead now – and the living: the Major, Sokolova and now Finch. She knows the name, of course she does. One of the circling contenders for the Chief's job. A blood-smeller in the dark water. A man with a plan for his own career as much as for NATO. Creating the unmet need among the public and politicians that only his particular machinations can sate. Calling on the entire military machine to rear up as one, spitting and foaming, demanding relevance. Weapons-grade information warfare unleashed on unsuspecting audiences. Leading them on, deeper and deeper, out of their depth, closer to war, until they wail for a saviour and their fear can be converted into hard cash.

And then Finch will appear, preening as per his name. A diminutive bird. So common in both Europe and Eurosiberia. A delicate foot in both camps. The man who will negotiate with Sokolova and broker a de-escalation, then liquidate her soon afterward for good measure: closing the door behind him, leaving no trace of their conspiracy. His star will rise so fast and so high as to be beyond the reach of even the Chief's liver-spotted grasp. Finch the peace-bringer. The hybrid aficionado. And all at the expense of his predecessor. Too close a call on the Chief's watch. Disaster only narrowly avoided. Why hadn't he seen it coming? Isn't that the very function of his job, to protect by anticipating? Or so Finch will have it.

But that would be to underestimate the adversary. Or is it friend, as Nikolai and Dmitry would have her believe? A nation not averse to dying in their millions for nothing more than an idea. Is this a sufficient hill for them? The altar of freedom. An idea for which they have fought before but have chosen so wilfully to reject in peace.

Then again, maybe the Chief has known about Finch all along. About his plan and its perilous presumptions. The hidden fault line that runs deep beneath the glittering surface. Maybe he called her exactly because he understood: to stop the inevitable debacle that would ensue if Finch underestimated the Russians, as so many have done before. The Chief as augur several moves ahead: protecting by anticipating. Or then again, maybe he is just protecting his job.

The captain is speaking over the intercom. Clemmie blinks herself back from the lake of unresolved thoughts, into the turbulent present. They have started their descent.

Chapter Thirty-Four

Pipe smoke hangs in the air like an old-fashioned calling card. They find the Chief in the bedroom with the storyboard, staring rather dismissively at its inaccurate interconnections.

"Can I assume that Moscow helped you make more sense of this?"

Clemmie sighs into the chair beside him. Louise and Stig head for the main room to give them some privacy.

"Russians making sense, that would be something wouldn't it?"

"But they can be predictable."

"Why do I get the feeling that you've been working on that assumption all along?"

His eyes twinkle as he passes over the newspaper. The front page screams of war.

"He's been myopic about the region for years. A self-proclaimed subject matter expert, so no one questions his version of events."

"A *deskpert* who doesn't understand the Russian soul. Well, there's a surprise."

"He thinks Gogol's something Russians wear to go

swimming."

They enjoy the joke for a moment.

"The Ambassador in Riga: one of his? Is that why he wouldn't give us access?"

"More than likely."

"So, is there even an appetite to stop this?"

"Christ no, not in the slightest. Currently, everyone benefits. The Alliance, Global Britain blah blah. He's read the room; I'll give him that."

"But you still want us to…?"

"Yes."

"And you're sure it won't be seen as, you know…?"

"Saving my own skin? Of course it will. They'll be queuing up to give me a thorough kicking."

"As long as I've made you aware of the consequences."

"We'll stop him because it is the right thing to do. Can't tolerate renegades in our own ranks. Who knows where it'd end? Think of the precedent. And anyway, if we don't, we're in the hands of the Ruskies, God forbid. And I wouldn't put anything past them."

"You think they'll refuse to de-escalate?"

"Think? I *know*. They've never walked away from a fight in their history. And this time, just to help our greedy generals get a bigger slice of pie?" He laughs at the thought as he wheezily gets to his feet but gestures at Clemmie to stay in her seat. "And what is your assessment?"

"If they learn it's Finch, they'll recognise his audacity, but also his oversight. He's entirely driven by ego, and that could be useful to them, if he…" She trails off out of respect. The Chief shares none of her qualms and is quick to finish her sentence. "If he gets my job."

"Yes,"

"So, your assessment is that, if they learn of Finch, they will likely pull back, if only to promote him?"

"That's not what I said."

"But it is what you meant."

She chides herself silently for allowing the conversation to take this course. "I just think you need to be careful, that's all."

He detects the tenderness in her eyes and makes sure to return it. "In the fridge."

"The fridge?"

"The plan."

"Oh, a plan?" She laughs for ever having doubted him. "And is this an 'in response' plan, or was this always 'the plan'?"

He is already at the door. "Along with some oysters. Natives." He gives her a last knowing look on his way out. "Be sure to crush them up when you're finished. The oysters."

"Yes sir."

Chapter Thirty-Five

Alexander Finch is everything a grizzled high-flyer within the services should be. Thin greying hair that is longer than is either fashionable or reasonable, beaky yellowing teeth with receding gums due to a combination of smoking and unfortunate genes, and an air of constant distraction, as if considering something of significantly more importance than the matter in hand. He oversees the COBRA Committee meeting in the Chief's absence with barely concealed relish and a results-driven manner that has no truck with vagary. "And your assessment has been updated no doubt, in light of the new intelligence?"

The senior officer from the Defence Intelligence Staff is noteworthy, if only for his lack of memorability. A natural-born grey man. "Yes sir. The ground truth, as well as the motivational hypotheses have been reassessed."

"You got it wrong the first time, you mean?"

"I mean that posterior probability has now been taken into account."

Finch rolls his eyes with barely concealed contempt. "Fine, and what is your estimate now that you have had a chance to change everything retrospectively?"

"That the Russian intent is now overtly hostile. They can be assessed to have progressed to a war footing."

"Oh really? How remarkably-bloody-observant of you."

Finch sighs theatrically for the benefit of the wider audience. The central table, which he chairs, comprises various uniformed representatives from the armed forces, as well as an assortment of senior governmental lawyers and advisers, in person and on relay screens. A second battery of chairs encircles the first, populated by a team of junior officials who busy themselves taking notes and sending emails in response to the unfolding conversation. The sigh is duly noted.

Finch turns to one of the screens: "And SIGINT, what do the good folk of Cheltenham surmise? Something a little more enlightening, I would hope?"

A tight-faced redhead provides her clipped assessment: "Yes sir, we have satellite and communications product to indicated self-propelled howitzers and BMP-3 infantry fighting vehicles moving into the area, supported by logistics and approximately six thousand troops. They aren't even pretending that this is an exercise."

Finch widens his eyes at the DIS officer, to ensure that the lesson is learnt. "Clear, tangible and actionable. Thank you, Cheltenham."

The room waits as Finch sips at his water before continuing. He replaces his glass slowly, to build the tension. "So, what do we, collectively, make of that? The Prime Minister requires our recommendations."

A tough, short-haired man in military uniform is the first to speak: "They are undermining the entire de-escalation agreement."

"Indeed, General. Acute and succinct as ever. Anyone else?" He turns in the direction of a smart preppy adviser at the far end of the table. "Perhaps a political perspective?"

"Cabinet will take your lead on this, out of deference to your position as a subject matter expert."

The sycophancy isn't misplaced. Finch visibly grows in his chair. "Thank you, Mark." He nods to another uniformed man. "So, they are in advanced preparations for outright war, is that what I am hearing?"

"From our current intelligence picture—"

With a theatrical sweep of his hair, Finch interrupts: "Is that a yes or no, Admiral?'

"It's a yes."

Finch points at the others in turn. "In the interests of brevity please: corroborated, yes, or no?" The other key stakeholders all gesture their affirmation. "Well, there we have it. A serious turn of events indeed. But we know from history, do we not, that we must not shirk from Russian aggression. In all my years studying the region, I can say with some degree of knowledge," with a smile to Mark, "perhaps expertise even, that the Russians do not understand, or respect, enervation in others. Well, am I right?"

Without anyone knowing the meaning of enervation, he gets shrugs rather than nods. This evident disappointment elicits another of his grand sighs. "And let us not be, as trusted representatives of our country at this difficult time, the kind of men and women that history will judge to have been enfeebled, or heaven forbid equivocal. Am I also right?"

This time, there are nods, albeit with scratching of heads, as they grapple with Finch's elaborate sentence structure. "So be it. Our collective decision is made. We petition NATO to respond in kind, with immediacy and fortitude."

The grey man coughs. "But sir, isn't that the decision of the Prime Minister alone?"

This takes the wind out of Finch's sails momentarily before he snaps back: "And did you seriously think I wouldn't be speaking with the PM immediately after this meeting? Assuming he isn't predisposed with more pressing matters of state? Was that another of your wrongful assessments?!" The DIS officer, having lost a further shade of colour from his face, is spared further embarrassment by the emergence of a young Personal Private Secretary behind Finch, who says: "Actually, he's in with your

Head Shed at the moment, sir."

One of Finch's wispy eyebrows raises at this news. He grabs at the man's arm over his shoulder and pulls him close. "The Chief? With the PM?"

"Yes sir."

"And why was I not told?"

The young man doesn't have an answer. He tries to remove his hand. Finch is about to let go, when he notices the man's watch under his pressed white shirt, with its regimental canvas strap coloured in the blue and red of the Blues and Royals. He nods approvingly before also seeing the leather bracelets around the man's wrist. "And do get rid of those things. Where do you think you are, at a music festival?"

"Yes sir. I mean, no sir."

There is a pause as Finch regains his composure. "Well that's as it should be, am I right? The Chief will be forewarning the PM of our likely intent, I dare say. Meeting adjourned."

They exit the room according to seniority, although Finch remains behind, as does the redhead on the link from Cheltenham. "My eyes and ears, what else do you have for me?"

"Intercepts indicate that our NATO allies will support the recommendation, with no vetoes."

Finch takes another slow sip of water. "Of course they will."

Chapter Thirty-Six

The afternoon cooking shows are interrupted by the breaking news that NATO is dramatically increasing its militarisation along Russia's southwestern border in response to alarming troop movements within the Federation. Clemmie mutes the coverage.

A new storyboard now adorns the wall, with a photo of Finch on one side and Sokolova on the other. Gone are the pictures of corpses. The entire pictogram is now a representation of chains of command and the information distribution networks that the two sides have at their disposal, including the very BBC News channel they are currently watching. Stig makes a finishing touch to the assemblage. "Hasn't the PM called the Kremlin, to explain what's actually going on?"

"Almost certainly."

Stig gestures to the screen: images of fast jets conducting reconnaissance missions within NATO airspace. "He couldn't get through?"

Clemmie uses her mobile as a prop to simulate the conversation. "Hello, Mr President? Yes, it was a

NATO conspiracy that started all this after all, but we'd really rather not reap what we've sown if it's all the same to you?"

Louise enters. "Good luck."

"Exactly." Clemmie returns the phone to her pocket. "Why wouldn't they exploit it? It's clear to everyone they didn't start it. They'll play it for everything it's worth if they've got any sense."

The TV animations depict different scenarios, including the Russian annexation of various neighbouring countries. Louise shakes her head as she studies the images. "It could have been the deal that Finch made with Sokolova from the start. Why she would back his plan. A territory back for Mother Russia as the price for de-escalation?"

Clemmie seems impressed with the idea. "Which would finish the Chief off once and for all. And China, India and the US would all agree to it if it guaranteed the much-needed peace deal. Oh, that's very good."

Stig scratches his head. "Hang on, if that's right, then with Finch's plan, everyone does actually win? No one goes to war. The Russians get their pound of flesh in the form of a former territory. NATO secures a new mandate, with increased commitments from the member countries. The PM re-establishes a new geopolitical authority for Britain. And Finch is crowned as the peacemaker and leverages that for good in the region, and maybe globally. So why can't it happen?"

"Because the Chief doesn't think they'll stop – the Russians – when Finch tells them to, through Sokolova."

"But he doesn't know that."

"Well of course not."

"He just 'thinks'?"

"The Chief, Stig. Not some recruit. He anticipates that when Finch gives the order to de-escalate, it will be ignored."

"And he thinks that because?"

"Because they are already onto Sokolova, so they will have the means to change the game whenever they want, however they want."

"That presupposes they will try and screw us. What if he's wrong?"

"And what if he's right, Stig? What if they don't stop after the first annexation? Assuming that was the agreed price with Finch. What if they get a taste for it, and they expand a bit further? Maybe a few overthrows in the Middle East, how about then?"

"So, we'll never trust anyone: that's the Chief's answer? Isn't that what got us into this mess? A total lack of trust on all sides? For decades. No viable peace in the region because everyone *thinks* everyone else is trying to screw them over. Maybe that's exactly why Finch resorted to what he's been doing: because it's the only way to work around the Chief's bitter old cynicism?"

Clemmie pleads as she tries to get Stig to see sense. "The Russians know we aren't geared for a hot war. They know it was never really Finch's plan. It's not like the Chief's taking a wild stab in the dark now, is it? Of course, the Russians will be looking to exploit this."

Stig shrugs petulantly. "It's a stab alright, just in their back!"

Clemmie shakes her head with exasperation: "Are you serious?"

"You said yourself how brilliant Finch's plan is."

"Yes, if it wasn't so likely to fail."

"There you go again. 'Likely to fail.' Says who? An old duffer who can barely breathe?"

Clemmie's jaw drops. "I'll pretend I didn't hear that, shall I?"

"Maybe there's some sense in him making way for some fresh blood, that's all I'm saying."

Clemmie seethes. Louise busies herself tidying imaginary papers to keep out of the way.

"Oh, is that so, Stig?"

Seeing her visceral anger, he tries a different tone. "Look, I didn't sign up to undermine my own side when it seems they're – we're – doing the right thing. Finch's plan leads to peace, why aren't I allowed to say that? Granted in the wrong way, but that's not exactly unusual for this line of work, is it?"

"The means do matter, Stig. We don't just let the Chief hang and walk away. 'I'm alright Jack, so fuck you', is that it?"

"This isn't about the Chief! At least, it shouldn't be. He's a busted flush. Everyone knows it. That's why they're all jockeying. Finch and the rest. But he's refusing to budge. You're the only one who seems not to be able to see that; for Christ's sake."

"Oh, for 'Christ's' sake now? So, hanging the Chief out to dry, that would be the Christian thing to do, would it?"

"What the hell has this got to do with belief?!"

"Well, it's as good a place to start seeing as we're discussing morals, and standards, and right and wrong!"

"We're discussing a job! A paying job, that's all!"

Stig hears his own words and is immediately ashamed. The room falls silent.

"Ah, money."

"I'm sorry. I didn't mean that. Not like that."

"No, you did. Own it. You said as much from the start. You need the money. So, take your pieces of silver and get out, you Judas!" Clemmie hurls the nearest object across the room, then suddenly regrets it. She raises her hands, recognising she has crossed a line. "Okay, I'm sorry." The damage has already been done. Stig stares back at her, forlorn. "I'm sorry, Stig, I apologise. I just got angry."

Louise picks up the object, a stapler, and whistles under her breath. The TV screen continues to play behind them. Putin is on screen, holding forth. Clemmie approaches Stig and places her hand on the back of his neck. "I want all your conviction, but focused in the right way."

Stig isn't listening; he stares at his feet, utterly ashamed of himself. "What if you're right?"

Clemmie continues with her point. "Defending liberal democracy: sure that governments and militaries should only ever act within the law. That's what I want you passionate about."

Stig speaks to himself. "I would have left the Chief to them."

"The priest, the lawyer, Ksenia: he must be held to account. Because that's what we stand for. All black and white. No grey areas on that. And we will do what is right exactly because of our faith, in the Chief. Are we clear?" He shrugs. "And if for any reason you don't agree with that, Stig, then now is your time to leave."

This final barb surprises him. He looks up into her eyes for clarification but gets only unwavering intensity in return. "We've been around this once before. Decide who you are going to be, Stig, once and for all."

Chapter Thirty-Seven

Father Gregory finds Stig on his knees in front of the life-size depiction of Jesus, at the eastern end of the cathedral's right hand aisle. A single candle is already halfway burnt down in a nearby sconce. Rather than interrupt, the priest takes a seat behind Stig on one of the wooden chairs that line the wall. Finally, when Stig gets to his feet, he is there for him.

"Father Lev told me that you had become a more frequent visitor."

"That's right."

"Also, that you were accommodated by our Latvian brethren."

"Your help was very much appreciated, thank you."

"Can I enquire as to your progress?"

"We are doing everything we can to protect the reputation of the Church at all stages of our investigations."

"I meant your spiritual progress, Bryan, isn't it?"

"Actually, no, it isn't."

"Progressing, or Bryan?"

"That's not really my name. I'm Stig."

The priest nods sagely, as if having always suspected the deception. "So, why are you here?" He watches as Stig wrestles, almost physically, to find the right words.

"Well, today, earlier, I…?"

"Confessing is embarrassing, yes?"

"Yes."

"Good, then you will want to reduce the number of times you commit the sin."

"I guess."

"So?"

"Today, I put money over loyalty. I made the wrong call."

"Ah, Judas!"

Stig stares back at him, stunned. "And that is meant to help, is it?!"

"But it's true, yes? You just said so. You are a Judas!"

Shamed, Stig nods. Father Gregory roars with laughter, then places his hand on Stig's shoulder. "And you came here because you wanted to make it all go away, yes? The guilt? The shame? That is why you are here?"

"Well, not exactly but…"

"Of course it is!" The priest walks over and gestures to the depiction of Christ. "You think he is Harry Potter, maybe? With a magic wand? Abracadabra, and it all goes away?"

"That's not what I…"

"Let us see." Gregory takes the large cross from his chest, holds it like a wand, and waves it violently in Stig's face. "Abracadabra! So, did that work? Are you less ashamed now, Stig? Here, again, abracadabra!"

Another bellow of laughter. Stig remains stoic, although clearly humiliated. "I thought I could talk to…" He gestures back to the figure of Christ. "That's all."

"What, and now you can't even say His name. To Jesus? You thought you could talk to Jesus Christ about being a Judas, yes?"

"Yes, to Jesus…Christ."

"And you thought that Jesus Christ would want to hear your whining? With everything else going on in the world?" He affects a childish voice. "Poor me, Jesus Christ; I am Judas, Jesus Christ; do your magic for me, Jesus Christ."

"I get it."

"If you want Harry Potter, you should go to a cinema, not to a church."

More angrily now: "Yes, I get it!"

Father Gregory steps close and stares, unblinking, into Stig's eyes. "So why are you still here?"

"How do you mean?"

"You should leave. You got the wrong building, yes? Leave."

He gestures towards the door, but Stig doesn't move. The priest softens his tone. "Ah, so you want to do this again, but properly now?"

"Yes, I would like that, please."

"'Step away from the others and I shall tell you the mysteries of the kingdom. It is possible for you to reach it, but you will grieve a great deal.' You know who said that?"

"Jesus?"

"To Judas. It's apocryphal, but clear I think, yes?"

"Yes."

"So, what does it mean?"

"It means…" Stig flounders.

"It means our grieving is because we are just human. We are Judas, and Samson, and Eve and Tamar. We will always fall short, but we must try to live up to Him. You're only human. He knows that."

"So, what should I do?"

The priest laces his arm around Stig's neck and pulls him close, to whisper into his ear, "Stop wasting His time, and yours." Taken aback by his manner, Stig tries to pull away, but the priest yanks him closer with more force. "Look up."

Stig raises his eyes slowly to the ceiling. Father Gregory points him to a series of murals high above them. "This wasn't originally a Russian cathedral, but we still recognise the saints of course." Stig can just discern the figure of Jesus carrying the cross in one alcove, with two saints pictured above. One of these figures is wearing armour, the other sackcloth and bindings. "Top left. That's Saint Oswald. King of Northumbria. One of the early believers, and one of the most powerful rulers your country has ever had. At least, according to Bede. Have you heard of him?"

"No."

"He used his influence wisely to spread Christianity. Through persuasion, not battle. Sound familiar?" Stig nods bashfully at the comparison. "Now, read it to me."

Straining his eyes, Stig just manages to make out the weathered English text to the right of the soldier-king, "'Be strong…'"

"Yes, and under that?"

"'And play the man.'"

The priest guides Stig's attention back to him. "That's right, 'be strong and play the man'. No more whining about your own fallibility. It's about what you do with what you have. Your talents, am I making myself clear?

"Yes, Father."

"Be the Church, don't just visit it." He gestures Stig back to the area on the floor where he was previously praying. "Now, get back down there on your knees and ask for guidance, not forgiveness. You may be surprised what happens then." With this, Father Gregory releases his grip. He brushes down his vestments and then, after a curt smile and bow, continues his tour of the cathedral, searching out any other worshippers who may be hiding in the shadows. With a sigh, Stig traipses back over to the figure of Christ and gets down on his knees.

Chapter Thirty-Eight

The Chief is in his office. There is a knock at the door. "In."

Finch enters with a breezy confidence and takes the only available seat. The Chief finishes signing a document without looking up. Finch notices the green ink with a sour smile to himself; the exclusive preserve of the serving Chief. He studies the old man's hands. A mosaic of the particular browns that only come with age and frailty. He sees the dandruff on the lapels of his pinstripe jacket. No doubt because those old hands are too feeble to wash the thinning hair with due vigour. The wheezing, rasping, breathing. A portrait of decrepitude. Finally, the Chief raises his eyes and is met by Finch's warm smile. "Alexander. A drink?"

"Thank you, no."

"And how are we today?"

"Top of the world. Yourself, Chief?"

The Chief coughs to himself, then gestures that this is his answer.

"The pipe is helping though, no?"

A slight raise of the Chief's fingers from the table.

He reaches for water. Finch waits until the drinking ritual is over before continuing: "This is about the Ruskies no doubt?"

"Indeed."

"The PM saw sense, of course. Little choice, given the evolving intelligence picture."

"Quite so. Conflict seems inevitable."

"A classic Bayesian revision. One for Training Wing in due course."

"Indeed."

The Rev. Bayes' rule for calculating posterior probability: the evolution of one's intelligence estimate according to new information. As relevant today as it ever was, with enough lessons to be learnt on this occasion to warrant a fuller conversation between the who men. But not today. This is an altogether different meeting.

"And your assessment, Alexander?"

"Of the veracity of the intelligence? First-class by all accounts. GCHQ rating it highly."

"I would expect nothing less."

Finch smiles graciously, unsure as to whether the compliment was for him or GCHQ, but happy either way.

"And now I hear there's talk of us losing Ukraine?"

"We await the exact nature of Russia's ambitions in response to this supposed conspiracy that they've cooked up."

"Quite so. But your assessment, Alexander?"

"I've just provided it for you, Chief," he says with a condescending glint, as if humouring an old relative.

"Of course you have." Another theatrical pause for water. An intangible sense that the Chief is aware that Finch borrowed this same technique for his recent COBRA meeting.

"And your assessment, Alexander?"

"Chief? I beg your pardon?"

"Your assessment. Of the likely outcome?"

"Are you feeling alright, sir? Is there perhaps something I can get you?"

"How do you mean?"

"That is the third time you have asked me the same question. About my assessment of the situation?"

"Ah, yes. So, what is it then?"

"What's what?"

"Your assessment of the situation, Alexander?"

Finch is about to provide another exasperated reply, but the Chief's sudden bout of coughing stops him in his tracks. This time, the retching from across the table does not immediately abate. Finch winces as he watches the old man holding onto the table to steady himself as he struggles for breath.

"Chief, if that will be all?"

"Yes, thank you Alexander, very useful." He waves him away and returns to his writing.

Finch is by the door before he turns back. "In fact, Chief, one thing?"

"Certainly, Alexander, a drink?"

"Chief, perhaps you wouldn't mind if I took the lead on this? I think it wouldn't be self-aggrandising for me to say that I know the region rather better than many, most, in this building?"

"Lead what?"

"Our Russian response."

"Ah."

"The assessment that I provided to you, just now, well perhaps you would agree to this course of action and task me to act upon it?"

"Assessment?"

"Yes, Chief."

Finch watches as the old man searches his memory and seems happy with what he finds. "Yes, very good. Very proactive. I'd expect nothing less."

"So, I have your authority, Chief? To handle this my way?"

"Authority, and my highest esteem, Alexander. Safe hands in serious times. 'You can't imagine how stupid the whole world has grown nowadays.'"

"Nice line, Robert Browning?" But the Chief is already away in his mind and onto other matters.

Finch leaves without waiting for a reply.

Once alone, the Chief closes his fountain pen and screws the lid tightly. He stares at the closed door, as he speaks quietly to himself. "Not Browning. Gogol. Nikolai Gogol."

He reaches for his water, briskly this time, and downs the rest of the glass.

Chapter Thirty-Nine

Clemmie passes through security and is greeted by Nikolai.

"The Ambassador is away this afternoon. Perhaps you would enjoy a little more space for our conversation?"

He shows her into the grand main reception room, rather than the wood-panelled antechamber of her previous visit. Ceiling-high double doors give way to a sizeable cream-walled interior with an assortment of the most fabulous Russian artistic treasures in ornate gilt-edged frames on every wall. There are the rarest Byzantine tapestries, vast seascapes by Ivan Aivazovsky and delicate figurative portraits from the height of the Empire. Clemmie makes no attempt to hide her wonderment.

"Yes, we certainly have a history to match any. Perhaps too much history for our own good." Nikolai has lost none of his diplomatic charm. He gestures for her to sit at the large, long table in the centre of the room, facing the stone balcony and scrupulously maintained gardens beyond.

"He certainly knows how to live: the

Ambassador." An aide enters with tea and slices of lemon, and they each accept a cup. They wait in formal silence until the tea is poured and they are alone again before continuing. "I wanted to thank you for Moscow."

Nikolai waves away the idea. "I've no question that you would have done the same for me, had our positions been reversed."

They both know this not to be true, so get down to business.

"I mean no discourtesy to you, Nikolai Ivanovich, but, given the seriousness of events, I was rather hoping to see the Ambassador as well."

"An unpredictable diary during these unprecedented times. I will have to suffice."

Clemmie draws herself up in her seat. "We cannot allow you to do this."

"To do what?"

"Annexation. Multiple annexations, if that's what you're planning?"

"And who said anything about…?" Her glare cuts him short. "And when you say 'we', are you perhaps speaking for NATO?"

"You know I'm not."

"But I think I am correct in saying that NATO is likely to agree to us reclaiming what is rightfully ours? In the name of peace?"

"I have the Chief's authority to stop you."

"Ah, your Chief. Not in the rudest of health, is he?"

"He's just fine."

"Barely able to hold a conversation, I have it on good authority."

"And *his* authority is as strong as it ever was."

He smiles to avoid any escalation of their own. "We should really be having it with a spoonful of jam: the tea. So much better than lemon. The true Russian way. Of course, you know this already. But did you know that we had Mr Finch here for tea earlier today?"

"'We'?"

"Ah yes, the Ambassador was able to attend that meeting. Unpredictable, as I said."

"And what did the Ambassador and Mr Finch discuss?" Gesturing to her tea. "Sweeteners?"

He enjoys her joke. "Quite so. A refreshingly enlightened man. I have no doubt he will go far."

"No."

"No?"

"Whatever Finch has promised you. No. He doesn't have the authority."

"That may not be entirely accurate as it happens. It seems he is a man who gets what he wants. We respect that."

"Sokolova is his asset."

"Yes, we know. And he seems to have run her very effectively. Look at what they have achieved."

"Embarrassing for Russia, if that were ever to come out?"

"Is that a threat?"

"It's a statement of fact."

"She will be dead as soon as we find it convenient. That is also a statement of fact. Naming her would only bring that date forward." He smiles over his teacup. "You didn't seriously think that would work, did you?"

Chastened, she tries a different tack. "Then we'll burn Finch too. Russia being played like a fiddle by a second-rater within our service. Not even our Chief. Can you imagine what the world would say? That Russia isn't even able to cope with our second team?"

He laughs to himself. "Well, as enjoyable as it would certainly be to watch you trying to explain away a rogue within your own service, I'm not sure that strategy would even achieve your desired intent, would it? You would simply be providing us with even more evidence of a conspiracy at the heart of NATO. It would further legitimise our own position and actions." He sips as he studies her. "Is that all?" She doesn't respond. "Then, if I may say, I think what you are revealing to me here is that your position is very weak."

She winces at the accuracy of his appraisal. Dmitry

had been right to rate him.

"You can't do this. Morally."

"I don't think I'd be overstepping the mark to say that the Kremlin doesn't fully align with your *individual* assessment of the situation. Morally, it is in our rights to respond to this provocation."

"Did he promise you Ukraine?"

He seems affronted by the directness of her question. "It would be rather unforgivable for us not to use this unfortunate situation fully to our advantage, don't you agree?"

Clemmie has no further ideas. She gets up with a sigh and walks over to survey the gardens. The first of the roses are in bud, although it is too early to tell whether they will bloom red or white.

"Will you stop, when Finch says?"

"Not immediately."

"But if he doesn't secure his peace deal, then no promotion. He'll be of no further value to you, surely?"

Another soft laugh and smile from Nikolai. "Nice try."

"But it's true."

"With what we have on him, he will be more useful to us the higher he flies. That is certainly true. Peace will need to be negotiated in his name, but in due course. There's no rush; the reality is you aren't ready for war, and we both know that."

"And then you will have everything you ever wanted: your Empire, and our top dog on a short leash."

He opens his palms as if to give thanks. "We can only play the cards we are dealt. It is nothing personal."

She turns back to face him. "Then there is nothing more to say, other than congratulations. I'll see myself out."

He stands as she leaves, then retakes his seat and refills his cup, smiling. But, just as Clemmie passes through the immense double doors, she catches sight of it: the icon on the wall. Sixteenth-century, perhaps even earlier. Priceless, no doubt. She can just make out an angel holding a sword, although the pigment is so aged that the image is barely intelligible. But its significance for her is, anyway, beyond the literal. Her eyes narrow as she turns slowly back to face Nikolai. She speaks with a new cold assurance: "The non-possessors."

There is a momentary tremble within his smooth exterior. "I'm sorry? Is that meant to mean something?"

"We'll make this all about the Church."

A double blink, then a pause, then a forced laugh. "Oh don't be so ridiculous, please sit down." She remains standing. Nikolai adopts a more jovial manner to try and break the deadlock. "Don't be unreasonable, Clemency, we have been through too much together in recent weeks."

"You know I will. We will. Not just radicalising one priest, like Finch did, but on an industrial scale. Historical proportions. NATO collaborators throughout Orthodoxy. A hotbed of dissidents. The non-possessors going head-to-head with the Patriarch of Moscow and all Russ. The Church ripping itself apart. The entire 'Church and state' authority you've been building for decades, at home and in the region, we'll make it cannibalise itself, and your power."

He refuses to play along with her and turns back to his tea, but Clemmie isn't finished. "And it'll play so well internationally. Religious fundamentalism. Feeding the suspicion and the fear. Russia as the true pariah. A threat to everyone."

"You can't be serious? This is a preposterous idea."

"The Ukrainian Church has already claimed independence. Priests were all over the Belarus protest movement. The dissent is already there. And that was just the start!"

He takes the bait and snaps at her. "You leave what you don't understand well alone."

"Coming from you?! Who recognises nothing as sacred?! Apart from power for power's sake. Look at what you've done. Politicising the Church. And they know it. Every believer. It confirms their lived experience. You bullying the *have nots* and promoting the *haves*. They know you must be stopped, but they're afraid. Now we will support them. And they will fight you in God's name."

"If you poke a bear, you will get bitten. I warn you."

"Is that a threat?"

"It is a fact. Don't make the mistake of finding out for yourself, Clemency. You want to undermine us from within? And then what? And overthrow the Patriarch and the President? And who will you get? Someone more pro-China. Maybe better the devil you know, yes?"

Clemmie laughs openly, harshly, into his face. "Listen to yourself. By your own admission, who you are." He waves her away. "You know I will do this. For every annexation, for all the land you grab, you'll lose the hearts and minds of the people. Because we'll show that you betrayed the Church for your dreams of Empire."

"No one will believe you."

"They'll believe it because it's the truth. Every congregation, in every church. They can see it for themselves. The fat possessors with their limos and blackedout windows, making promises to the poor only for the next life, not this. The very people you were meant to help: Church and state. And we'll be there, stoking it up. Religious fervour. More

267

passionate than any politics. Poisoned chalice doesn't come close to describing it. The mess you'll have on your hands. Until they sweep aside your earthly authority. Cleansing the temple. In God's name. It'll make 1917 look like a dress rehearsal." She laughs at the sheer magisterial beauty of her own idea.

He stands purposefully, as if to end the conversation, then walks to the window. When he does speak, his voice is calm but strained: "A fascinating thought experiment, granted. Possible even, but certainly not appropriate. I'm sure that you wouldn't wish to debase the gentility for which your service is so rightly renowned."

He turns to face her. Silhouetted against the windows, all that can be seen is his smile. "Let us return to a more refined footing, shall we?" Gesturing to the table, "Please, in both our interests."

She crosses the room slowly as if to retake her seat, meets his smile with her own, then sweeps the entire tea service onto the floor in one violent arc of her stick. The crash of cups, saucers and bowls echoes around the artworks.

"We drink our tea with fluid sucked from a cow's tits. That's what fuelled our Empire. Don't make the mistake of believing that we are refined."

Chapter Forty

Stig stares at Clemmie in open-mouthed disbelief. "Say that again."

"It's their Achilles' heel. Their only one."

"Are you doing this…? I mean, is this because of what I said about the Chief?"

Clemmie is clearly affronted by the question. "Stig, this is entirely professional."

"You are suggesting we destroy their Church?"

"Implicate, not destroy. And probably not. Hopefully not, if that makes you feel better. The ball is in their court, but we need to prepare for every eventuality." Clemmie turns to also involve Louise in the conversation. "I want you both to get a press release written up, with all the evidence listed. Mark it as from NATO. They can say it's the result of an internal investigation."

Louise heads for her area of the main desk. "On it. You want to name Finch as well?"

"All of them. Everything that we have, as it happened."

"Right-o."

Louise gets busy, but Stig just stays standing

directly in front of Clemmie. She tries to pass him, but he steps into her path. "Do you know what this will do?"

Her steeliness is intentional and leaves nothing to the imagination. "Yes, I think I am fairly sure, Stig. It will drive a wedge between the Russian Church and the Russian state, which is foundational to the Kremlin's influence within the region, especially within the former states. It's a textbook *fissure* strategy, as you will no doubt have been taught during your training."

"To the normal people who go to church?"

"Well, it will hopefully create division. That's the general idea."

"You know exactly what I'm saying."

"Oh, you mean do I know how it will impact them spiritually? No, I can't say I do, Stig. But then, that's not my job, is it? Nor indeed my problem!"

"You will undermine the entire fabric of trust."

"Well, if a job's worth doing. Now get to work please." She forces herself past. He follows.

"What about secondary audiences; unintended consequences? They taught us about those in training too, you know."

With a sigh and evident frustration, she crosses her arms and prepares to have it out with Stig once and for all. "Well perhaps that trust fabric needs some unpicking anyway, wouldn't you say? Or do you seriously believe that the Russian authorities aren't already, and extensively, using the Church for their own purposes?"

"I have seen no evidence of that."

"Because you haven't bothered to look, Stig. Because you've been so swept up by all the incense and candles that you've forgotten who you are, and what you are. An operator. Being asked to put together a fissure campaign. Just like many other operators at this exact moment in time, on jobs just like this one, in other geostrategically important areas around the world. And all of them I don't doubt, with bosses who are a lot less patient than me!"

"This isn't right, and you know it."

"Fissure strategies are effective, Stig. That's why we use them: as a means to an end."

"Before, you said the means didn't always justify the end. When we were talking about the Chief. So, which is it?"

"That was different."

"Why?"

"Because this is the Russians and the mission. Not a hare-brained side hustle by a deranged egotist who risks starting a war while simultaneously trying to undermine the head of our service. Are you being intentionally stupid?"

He doesn't hide his anger, but Clemmie is also far from happy. "Or do you suggest that we let the Russians annex the hell out of the region?"

"No, obviously not."

"Just to protect the reputation of an already-politicised religion?"

"I said no."

"Good, because that would be, quite frankly, insane. We owe nothing to this Church, apart from board and lodgings in Latvia, do we?"

"I guess not."

"And any personal spiritual awakening you may be having is exactly that: personal." Clemmie slumps into her chair. "So, there we are. The way it is. The Church is our only card, and we play it. Now get to work."

*

Finch oversees the construction of an elaborate briefing room. Union Jacks are being positioned on either side of a grand lectern, on a low stage, in front of rows of temporary chairs that stretch all the way to the back of the large interior. He ushers the junior members of his team this way and that with an ever-increasing degree of irritation. "No, not there! That'll be out of camera shot. Use your brain, or at least borrow someone else's."

*

Louise and Clemmie chat as they work. Stig opts

for silence. He has various files and papers scattered around him: a patchwork of evidence to illustrate the timeline of events. He takes a photo of each item in turn, then drops the images into the press release they are co-creating on the shared drive. Father Igor's rictus smile leers at him as he pastes the photo of the priest's corpse among the others. Clemmie ambles over. "You okay?"

"Why wouldn't I be?"

"I know this isn't what you would have wanted."

"We said we'd protect them. That was the deal. It's why Father Gregory gave us our first lead. To Latvia."

"I know."

"And now we're shafting them."

"You have to disconnect; stay mentally uninvolved. Step away, to get on with the job in hand." Clemmie can see that her choice of words has triggered something in Stig's mind. "What? What is it?"

He looks up at her, as if struck by a sudden realisation. "'Step away from the others and I shall show you the mysteries.' That's it."

"Stig?"

"You're right." Lost in his thoughts, he stands, grabs his coat and makes for the door. "That *is* what I have to do."

"And where are you going?"

He stops, remembers himself and returns to

Clemmie. He embraces her. "I'm so sorry. But I have to…"

Without explaining any further, he leaves. Clemmie and Louise stare at each other, dumbfounded, as they listen to his footsteps clatter down the stairs and out, the front door slamming behind him. Louise gets to her feet as if to follow. "Shall I?"

"No." Clemmie gestures her to retake her seat. "That's enough now. Let him go. It's his choice."

They both take a moment to collect their thoughts, before Clemmie returns to her desk. "Right, where were we?"

*

The feed to Moscow is established. Sokolova looks sternly at her image on the relay monitor. She checks her makeup, then her clothing, then the hastily constructed set behind her. She instructs a junior to move the Russian flag so that it is within the frame, with the same curt impatience as her British counterpart.

Finch seems pleased as he watches her from London. He snaps at the two operators controlling the sound and lighting from the back of the room: "Now show me the splitscreen. Come on, the two-shot, that's it." Their two locations, and images, are now shown on the screen for the first time, side-by-side. This is evidently going to be a joint statement.

*

Father Lev and Father Gregory are eating with a few other priests in the cathedral's icon-clad dining hall. Stig barges in and takes a seat opposite them. His stare is enough to tell them that this is serious, so Father Gregory smiles apologetically to the other priests. "Would you please excuse us, Fathers?" He places his hand on Father Lev's arm to keep him seated as the others dutifully leave them to it.

The old priest now fixes Stig with an unimpressed look. "Whatever the gravity of the situation, manners are never out of place in God's house. Am I making myself clear, young man?"

Stig laughs, as much in relief as in response to any humour. "Yes Father, you are making complete sense."

*

Finch and Sokolova are both at their positions behind their respective lecterns. The operators in each country adjust their shots to make the split-screen match perfectly. The images zoom in tight on each of them to focus, then pull back to their final mid-shots. Finch speaks into his microphone: "Testing, testing." Despite the glaring light in his eyes, he can just make out a thumbs-up from the back of the room, and now addresses Sokolova: "And can we get your levels please, Anna?" She speaks Russian into her microphone and simultaneous subtitles are generated on the screen below her, including a spelling mistake, much to Finch's annoyance. He shouts once again at the operators: "Use your fingers, not your knuckles!"

*

Father Gregory weaves his fingers together across his broad stomach and leans back with a serious air as Stig finishes what he has been saying. "And you are quite sure about this?"

"Yes. But it has to be now. Right now."

Father Gregory nods thoughtfully before finally turning to Father Lev: "And your feeling, Father?"

The younger priest takes a good look at Stig before speaking: "He is ready."

Stig blinks away a tear as he smiles his thanks to the two men.

*

"Let them in!"

In the glare of the lights, Finch stays standing by the podium as the doors to the room are opened and the press begin to pour in. He isn't able to make out exact faces, just the overall clamour of microphones being set up and people jostling for the best seats. He smiles to himself with the cool aloofness of a royal spectating the preparations ahead of their own coronation. His plan is reaching its crescendo and with it, he is adopting his final form. No longer in the queue for succession. This is the seizing of the throne. A process of self-actualisation on a grand scale. From hopeful to heritor. From deputy to Chief.

*

Stig stands, with a towel around his waist and Father Lev by his side, in front of a small lectern within the baptismal room. An antique silver-clad Bible rests open in front of him. "You must confess everything. Here and now."

Stig turns to look at him, a flicker of concern across his face. "What you are going to hear. It changes everything."

"I will hear nothing. But God will. You deal directly with Him now. I am here only as a witness, Stig. What would you like to confess, my child?"

Stig inhales deeply, then starts to speak.

*

Finch takes a deep breath to puff himself up and fill the screen, then sweeps back the unruliest strands of his long greying hair. He stares directly into the various cameras that are now trained on him as the room falls silent. He pauses, sips slowly from a glass of water to build tension and then speaks with all the gravitas he can muster: "Hello, and welcome to this simultaneous broadcast from London and Moscow. It is, of course, unusual, if not unprecedented, for a senior serving member of the intelligence services to make a media statement of any kind. Ours is, after all, a discreet profession." He pauses to ensure that, in the darkness behind the harsh television lights, the press has sufficient time to make a note of his every word. "However, these have been unprecedented times, and if the price for my role in this matter is a degree of notoriety, then so be it. We must each carry our own cross."

*

Stig's tears stream down his face as he comes to the end of his confession. Lev stares at the back of his head, askance. Stig turns to face him, barely able to look into the young priest's eyes. "I don't know what will happen. But I need you to know that I wanted to be here: on this side of it. Defending the Church. That is my choice."

Father Lev nods, although still completely shaken by the consequences of Stig's confession. "God sees that."

Stig still looks concerned. "And what I said; what you heard?"

"The Seal of Confession. It is not a matter for me, it is for God now."

"But *you*, Father. Can *you* forgive me?"

Stig watches the priest closely, for the first time seeing him as a young man; older than him, but nonetheless young. He searches his face for a sign, whether consternation or conciliation, but Father Lev remains entirely opaque. He just stares back with a lack of focus, as if communing with a different audience, a different agency. Finally, his attention refocuses on the man in front of him, and he smiles. "We are all only human. That's the whole point."

*

Finch's metamorphosis is happening on screen in real-time. He holds court with a previously unseen degree of poise. His florid language now feels appropriate, in keeping with the significance of the occasion, the topic and his awe-inspiring role in events. "The unthinkable consequences of a conflict with Russia were, of course, at the forefront of my mind as I opened discreet channels with the Kremlin."

The audience in the room remains still and entirely silent in the shadows, aware that their every sound risks being picked up by the many microphones and broadcast live to networks all over the world, in accordance with Finch's precise distribution instructions.

"It was, of course, a reputational risk for my employers, and myself individually. However, with seniority comes responsibility, and I personally, individually, assessed that the risk was worth the potential reward. I repeat that the recent tensions, had they not been addressed head-on, could have escalated uncontrollably towards an existential threat to the entire world. Our request for Russia to now cease its hostilities and withdraw from any further expansionist intentions is made on the very cusp of a war that must not be allowed to fully ignite."

Another reach for the glass of water to ensure that the enormity of his revelation is given the necessary time to germinate within the mind of every viewer. This man, this man alone, is their saviour.

*

Father Lev gestures Stig to the large font. "Now please, this way."

A small flight of tiled stairs leads down into the water. Stig pauses. He closes his eyes and breathes in deeply. The incense from the nave beyond the door. The beeswax of the candles. His smells now. No longer the other. Internalised. Finding a welcome home deep within him. Then the sounds. The distant whispering of two of the laity. The clattering of brass being moved into position, in preparation for the upcoming service. His sounds now. Resonating in his ears and head in ways far beyond the literal. And the touch. Nakedness as a sensation and as a humility. A oneness with the Church externally and internally. A new synthesis. He reopens his eyes and smiles. He removes the towel from his waist. Naked, he slowly eases himself down into the water as the priest takes his position at the edge of the font. When Stig is standing in the cool water, Father Lev places his hand on the crown of his head. "The servant of God, Michael, is baptised in the name of the Father..." By the time that Stig has registered the anomaly of his new, Church name he is already underwater. He resurfaces with clear confusion but is immediately pushed down again. "And of the Son." This time, he stays down longer, until Father Lev has to peer down to check on him. When he does finally break thorough the water's surface, it is anew, ready for his final submersion. "And of the Holy Spirit."

*

Finch stabs his finger against the lectern to literally drive home his points. "This is now the time for peace, and a time for a new, mutual understanding between our respective nations and institutions. It is with great sadness that we can all now see the degree to which the relationship between NATO and Russia, as well as our respective security services, was allowed to degenerate. The unfortunate situation that precipitated this recent escalation will, I am sure, be the subject of a full investigation in the coming months, if only to avoid its repetition."

The Chief has his office television tuned to the live broadcast. He claps slowly and cynically at the screen in response to Finch's blatant professional coup. "Couldn't resist it could you, old boy?"

The screen now splits into two. Sokolova appears at her lectern in Moscow, alongside Finch, as he continues his briefing. "It is at this stage in the proceedings that I would like to pay testament to the representative from the Kremlin who joins us now for this historic briefing: Miss Anna Sokolova, the Assistant to the Director of Public Affairs in Russia." Sokolova nods curtly to the camera but remains silent. "It would not be an exaggeration to say that Miss Sokolova has helped to change the course of history between our great nations, as well as between Russia and the entire NATO Alliance."

Sokolova's face twitches rather than smiles in close-up.

*

The room has fallen silent. The only sound is that of Stig's breathing as he stands, motionless, in the font. Long, deep breaths, as if taking nourishment from the air around him an insect, taking the time to strengthen its new exoskeleton.

*

Finch is wrapping up: "And what we have negotiated here is not only an end to the current tensions, although that in itself is a significant milestone. Rather, we have co-created a new bilateral understanding and agreement in relation to the defence of our entire regional interests." This gets the response Finch had been hoping for. He pauses to survey the darkened audience as they start tapping furiously into their laptops and mobile phones. "That's right. We find ourselves, here and now, on the threshold of an entirely new level of cooperation between NATO and Russia that was previously unthinkable."

*

With a sigh, the Chief gets slowly to his feet, just as there is a knock at his door. "In!" Clemmie enters, with Louise in tow. The Chief gestures to Finch on the screen. "You've been watching?"

Clemmie points to the Chief's reception room. "Yes, out there."

They all stand around the Chief's table, watching as Finch continues his grand finale. "And this new spirit of cooperation will, I hope, NATO hopes, and as Miss Sokolova will confirm now, Russia hopes, lead the way to an ever-greater integration of international defence efforts, culminating in the previously unthinkable invitation, by NATO, for Russia to join its alliance of peace."

Again, Finch takes a moment to enjoy the effect of his words on the assembled audience. Despite the dimmed lighting, he can make out a few of the genuinely shocked expressions and whispered exchanges.

The Chief turns to face the two women. "And that is that: the endgame." He uses the remote to switch Finch off. "I think we've heard enough, don't you?"

Clemmie shakes her head. "Russia, joining NATO?"

Louise is similarly stunned. "And I bet that worm Newton has a supportive statement from Riga already prepared."

Clemmie chips in. "Counter-signed by our Ambassador no doubt."

The Chief eases around his desk and makes for the door. "Ladies, shall we?"

*

Finch gestures towards his counterpart in Moscow: "And now, ladies and gentlemen, I would like to hand over to Miss Anna Sokolova who will detail the steps by which Russia will take its place alongside the community of democratic allies within NATO. Miss Sokolova…" The screen switches to a one shot of Sokolova. Finch uses the chance to take stock. He surveys the room with a new confidence: the master of the proceedings, but also of his own destiny. It is only a matter of time now. The plaudits that will come: some pre-arranged, like those from Nikolai Ivanovich at the Russian Embassy, and others from his colleagues who wish to ingratiate themselves with the new brush. Then, the secret meetings will be held. The agreed wording of his predecessor's letter of resignation. Culpable, but not needlessly cruel. Of course, the Prime Minister will then need to be consulted and his wholehearted approval shared with the press. Finch, the new custodian of the famous green ink. The man for the times.

*

The double doors leading from the baptismal font into the cathedral are opened. Stig is standing, now dressed in a thin cotton gown, holding a single candle in his clasped hands, facing into the nave. Father Gregory is waiting for him. Dripping water behind him, Stig approaches the old priest who dips his fingers into a worn ceramic pot and carefully draws a cross with chrism on Stig's forehead. "The seal of the gift of the Holy Spirit, amen."

*

Delighted with the way in which events are going, Finch looks out around the gathered press. Just then, however, he sees the hand of one of the camera operators from behind his equipment. The fingers dancing over the camera controls. The pressed white shirt, the regimental watch strap with the blue and red banding of the Blues and Royals, and those familiar leather bracelets. From the COBRA Committee meeting. The relay monitor registers Finch's sudden change of expression in tight close-up: a look of confusion, verging on horror.

*

With his eyes closed, Stig can only hear snippets of the chanting around him. Father Gregory applies oil to Stig's eyes, his chest, his hands and his feet. Father Lev reads aloud, fast and quiet: "Who through the baptismal font bestows heavenly illumination to them that are baptised; who has regenerated this Your servant bestowing upon him forgiveness of his voluntary and involuntary sins; do You lay upon him

Your mighty hand, and guard him in the power of Your goodness…"

*

Sokolova remains on the screen but doesn't speak. Finch stares this way and that, trying to peer through the glaring lights to make sense of the unfolding calamity. He sees that the mixing desk at the back of the room is now unmanned. The two controllers, who had previously borne the brunt of his shouting, are now standing by the room's main doors, as if to attention. Utterly confused, Finch looks back to the Moscow feed and sees Sokolova being led away by two men, heavy-set, with short hair. One is grey-eyed, the other brown.

*

Both priests take their positions in front of Stig. "We have called you Michael. That will be your Orthodox name. The leader of an army of angels, but also a servant. We hope that you find it appropriate."

Stig looks back at them, unable to control his tears. They spill from him with joy, but also with a new confident humility. "Yes, it is perfect. Thank you, Father."

Setting aside any further formalities, the two priests suddenly burst into laughter and embrace Stig. "Welcome, Michael."

Father Lev holds Stig by the shoulders so as to look deep into his eyes. "Now, we are under your

286

command, Michael, how best do we do God's work?"

*

The house lights are switched back up to full as the Chief enters, flanked by Clemmie and Louise. Finch can now see the full horror of it. The many faces that he would have recognised had it not been for the television lights shining so directly into his eyes, deftly controlled, no doubt, by the two operators on the control desk at the back of the room. The very men he had been lambasting all along for their lack of professionalism. The room falls silent as the Chief turns to the assembled audience: "Thank you, everyone. You will just be in time for lunch if you hurry along to the canteen. Shepherd's pie today, don't miss it."

The Chief's natural authority is clear to see as the supposed press pack leaves the room in a far more orderly fashion than when they entered. The difference is not lost on Finch, who remains alone at the lectern. Only when they are alone, aside from Clemmie, Louise and the two sentries by the door, does Finch speak. His voice is quiet, but with an unequivocal anger and determination: "It wasn't broadcast, was it?"

The Chief approaches Finch slowly. Clemmie and Louise stay close but leave enough room for the old man to run things the way he sees fit. "You inviting Russia to join NATO? No. Just recorded for our own purposes. For the endgame." The Chief looks around him. "I would have expected more situational awareness from someone of your seniority, but then…" He wags a finger at Clemmie as an acknowledgement of her role in the plan. "We assessed that your ego would cloud your judgement. Correctly, it would seem."

Finch's fury is white-hot. "You just can't stand it, can you?"

"Your betrayal?"

"Don't! Don't you dare twist this!" Finch storms to the edge of the stage. He spits his words with venom. "They want peace! Why would you stop that?"

"Because…"

"Let me tell you why. Because you, you bitter old bastard, are just like all the others of your generation, here and in Riga. With your condescension, your Cold War fantasies and your passive-aggressive doctrines. Because your entire careers have been dedicated to sabotaging lasting peace rather than actually achieving it." The Chief nods sagely but doesn't interrupt. "The incessant sabre-rattling along the Russian border. Funding every conceivable opposition party to stir unrest. Have you even looked at a map recently, seen the military installations encircling Russia? That's incitement, not conciliation!" He jabs his finger at the Chief with a visceral hatred. "You are everything that needs to change. But you won't. And more than that, you just sit there out of spite, like an old immovable overlord, suppressing anyone who risks showing that you've been wrong all along. Bitterness upon bitterness: a self-fulfilling cycle of hate and division."

Despite Finch's barely contained hostility, the Chief turns his back to him and calmly sits on the edge of the stage. "Well, it's good to finally hear your assessment."

"There you go again, with your self-serving superiority. Christ, you make me sick!"

"Of course, there is another way of interpreting the evidence."

Finch motions for him to continue, but with a mocking look in his eyes. "Go on then, convince yourself. Justify why, yet again, you've killed hope in the nest. Own it, go on you old bastard!"

Still entirely calm, the Chief meets Finch's stare. "It is just possible, Alexander, that they were not following your plan, but their own."

"Wrong again! I designed this. All of it. Not them. But those cataract of yours just won't see it, will they?"

"So, he didn't approach you, Nikolai?"

"No! I went to them. Is that so difficult for you to understand? In the interests of a concord, I was proactive. I did this. Not them. Me! I knew NATO would greedily want the money. That the PM would crave the status. That all of them would do it for their own self-serving reasons, but ultimately it would result in peace. And what's wrong with that?!"

Finch steps down from the stage and up close to the Chief. "I did this for peace. So don't you dare judge this, or me. You just can't stomach the idea that there is another way: a better way. Bravo. Turn the cameras on yourself. Let's have a record of the man who destroyed peace to save his own skin. Let's show it to the PM alongside my tape and see what he says. A managed de-escalation, or more of the same: an underfunded NATO losing a hybrid war that you say is actually peace! Let's go. Ask him!"

"I did."

The quietness of the Chief's reply knocks Finch. "What?"

"When you took the COBRA meeting. I asked him."

"But he was in favour of it?"

"He was." Finch stares at him sceptically. "I said that you might be about to deliver the impossible: a genuine long-term peace. I said that if you were right, then I would resign, without hesitation, and that he should feel entirely confident that he was handing the service over to the right man: to you."

Finch is dumbfounded. He looks around to find his bearings. To Clemmie and Louise. To the sentries. Then back to the Chief. "So why…?"

"The PM agreed with me that the Russian desire to split NATO could not be discounted as their true motivation."

"That's ridiculous. I have been working on this for years. I told you, it was my idea."

"But am I correct in assuming that Russia joining NATO was not in your original, rather brilliant, plan?"

"So what? It's a value-add. They came up with it to help, to show their commitment."

"When?"

"Why does that matter? They suggested it in good faith. A long-term commitment to peace. You should be thanking them, not trying to find another bloody way to poison this!"

The Chief looks almost sympathetically at the younger, larger, man before him. "When, Alexander?"

"The first they mentioned it, was…"

"Yesterday perhaps, when you had tea with the Ambassador and Nikolai?" Finch reels. "Is that a yes, Alexander?" The Chief watches him play back events in his mind. The gradual, growing, look of concern. "The PM, wisely, ordered for the game to play on. To reveal whether they would indeed suggest their joining NATO, as their real price for peace. A bigger prize than any annexation. We needed you to show us, Alexander." He gestures around him. "All this circus, just for that." Finch slumps down beside the Chief. He can't bring himself to speak. "You didn't include it in your plan at the start because you knew it would never happen. It would be too rich for the blood of the Estonians and Lithuanians, let alone Norway and the other Baltics. You knew that instinctively when you were thinking straight. You knew that even to mention the idea would split NATO, making it weaker, not stronger."

"But it was only an addition. Another thing they would do for peace."

The Chief puts his arm around Finch's shoulder. "They played you, Alexander. Not at the start, but then, that isn't the Russian way. Doubtless, when you first brought them your plan, they assessed it on its merits. And my God it had merits, Alexander. A masterpiece for peace. Too good to be true. So, they formulated their own plan around it. Just as a precaution of course."

"You don't know that."

"And then they waited. They let you play your game, and they waited. Drawing you deeper and deeper. And why wouldn't they? Because at every stage they got what they wanted. You killed their dissidents for them in London. You manufactured a real NATO conspiracy for them. You killed on Russian soil. You promised them an annexation as the price for peace. And then, when they had you fully played out, and out of your depth, they made their move. Just an addition. A value-add in good faith. And you opened the gates and invited it in. Without recognising it for the Trojan horse it was." Finch's mouth hangs open as he considers recent events. "Because you had already won, yes? Peace was assured. Your promotion was assured. At any other time, you would have seen that the addition would undermine the entire alliance. But you were already too deep." Saliva drips down from Finch's chin onto his trousers. "They owned you, Alexander, because they saw that you so desperately wanted to believe in good. Virtuous, no question. But that's not our job, is it?" Now steely, the Chief faces Finch man-to-man. "Because we are paid to look for the worst in people, Alexander, just like I did with you. Because, as unpleasant, and bitter, and condescending as that makes me, it's the job. You betrayed me for a peace that you never achieved, for a deal that would have undermined your own side and strengthened theirs: the enemy's. You failed, Alexander. Me, the service, and your country. And you failed yourself, Alexander. For what?"

Finch barely manages to formulate his words. "And now?" The Chief shrugs. "Am I being arrested?"

"No."

"I don't understand."

"We remain at peace. Despite your promises, there will be no annexations. Clemency found a way to get

293

the Ruskies to see sense on that. As for the murders, Ksenia demonstrably orchestrated each of them. No prosecution against you would stick. So, this entire episode will remain as it of course should. *Semper occultus*. Always secret."

"And Sokolova?"

"Russian soil, Russian business. Consider yourself lucky."

"I cannot continue to work here, for you."

The icy glint in the Chief's eye is momentary but nonetheless striking. "On that we can agree." He softens again. "Perhaps retirement? There's many a Parish Council that would value your undoubted skills." Finch grimaces at the thought. "Or maybe you would like to live out your days in Russia, like Philby? Listening to cricket on the World Service and missing home?" The Chief remains impassive as he gets to his feet. "Let me know whatever you decide. I'll be in my office all afternoon."

The Chief shuffles back out, leaving Finch to Clemmie and Louise. The intensity of Clemmie's glare as she approaches is enough to immediately put Finch on his guard. "Your file. You have to understand, at that stage, I had no choice…"

The strike from her walking stick creates a fleshy echo around the empty room. It hits Finch directly on the temple. His pain comes as an exhalation – like air from a balloon – rather than a scream as he collapses to the floor at her feet. Barely conscious, feeling for the blood that now streams from the side of his head, he just manages to pull himself up in anticipation of the next blow. Clemmie raises her stick once again, but Louise reaches up and grasps it. "That's enough."

Clemmie nods to the younger woman and pulls herself together. She is about to walk away, but instead approaches Finch once again. He looks up pitifully as she looms over him. "You know what I see when I look at you?" He can't answer for blood. "I see nothing. None of the notoriety you wanted. No results for all your effort. No legacy. No professional pride. Nothing. Just a betrayer. That is your purgatory: to know that you are nothing."

Clemmie turns and leads Louise out of the room. The sound of Finch's whimpering gradually fades away behind them, to nothing.

Chapter Forty-One

Clemmie walks slowly into the grand room. A large man in an exquisite suit stands from behind the ornate central table as she enters. She recognises him immediately, from his photos in the newspapers, from his passive-aggressive appearances on the TV news, and from the Chief's file. She pauses to look around. "I was expecting to see Nikolai."

"He has been..." He chooses his words carefully. "Returned to Moscow."

"I see." Clemmie is on her guard. She peers around the room to establish whether he is alone.

"It seems that there was a phone call from our cathedral here in London. Directly to the Kremlin. And during this call, it was agreed that Nikolai's very particular skills could be better used in the service of the Church, rather than politics. A period of penance, you could say." He watches intently as the slightest smile appears at the edge of Clemmie's mouth. "And you know what's doubly strange?" Clemmie shrugs for him to continue. "Miss Anna Sokolova had the exact same thing happen to her. A re-tasking from the Kremlin to support the Orthodox Church in its many good deeds in Ukraine. I don't suppose you could shed any light on either of these interventions?"

Clemmie notices the icon of Archangel Michael staring back at her silently from the wall. "Sounds to me like the non-possessors also have friends in high places." She crosses the room and extends her hand. "Ambassador." He bows respectfully. His scent is as expensive as his tailoring.

"At your service. Tea?"

"With jam?"

"Lemon. The bitter taste seems somehow more appropriate today, at least for my palate."

She smiles as she crosses the room to survey the garden. The roses have started to bloom. They are red. "The irony is that you were right."

He joins her by the French doors holding two cups. "Please explain."

"Russia joining NATO is the only way to de-escalate this, in the long term."

"If you believe that, well then why—?"

She interrupts him. "Ends and means." She takes the tea. "Thank you."

He sighs as he watches a small, yellow-green finch use the garden's stone birdbath to preen itself before flitting away to be lost again within the nearby vegetation. "After so many years of trying, and failing... Well, you can perhaps forgive us for taking the opportunity to try something a little more imaginative on this occasion?"

"So close, too."

"And can I ask what has become of our dear colleague, Mr Finch?"

"Retired."

"Retired?"

"Not in the Russian way. A cottage by the sea."

He raises his cup. "To absent friends, then."

She looks closely into the pale liquid. "One thing, Ambassador?"

"Yes?"

"I need to know, are we back to civil relations?"

He laughs into the air. "You personally, you mean? Having ruined our entire plan?"

"Yes." She continues to wait before taking a sip. He has not yet drunk the yellow liquid either. Finally, pointedly, he drinks deeply from his cup. "Entirely civil. In fact, I could only wish to have someone with your professionalism on my own staff. Someone who also believes in our peaceful ends."

She nods away the compliment, as well as his attempt to recruit her. "Thank you, but I work for only one Chief."

"And he is lucky to have you, if I may say?"

She takes a large sip of tea, to his evident satisfaction, and they stand, enjoying the view. Her voice is quiet: "Why didn't you take what was on offer? 'A bad peace is better than a good quarrel.' Isn't that the Russian proverb?"

"We also say, 'Peace lasts until the army comes, and the army lasts until peace comes.'" He turns to look at her with a new intensity in his eyes despite his polished diplomatic manner. "NATO doesn't want peace, or they would allow us to join their alliance. All that was on offer was a different kind of war. With Finch's plan, nothing would have changed, ultimately."

"It was a start."

He shrugs. "You were prepared to use our Church against us because you assessed that it was the one thing we would not be prepared to sacrifice for this goal." She shrugs back. "But, if I am right, Clemency, your assessment was not based on the same textbooks and intelligence reports that people like Finch chose to read. Textbooks that describe the modern Russian Orthodox as just the latest way we subjugate our people, after communism."

"I can give you plenty of examples."

"But I don't think you believe that. Because I think you understand us well enough to know that we may just be sincere in wanting to protect and promote our Christian values. And whether you agree with our beliefs or not, you do at least respect conviction. As you did with, Stig, I think was his name?"

"That's a lot of assumptions, Ambassador."

"Because I think you recognise that, were we sincere in our beliefs, we would have done the exact same things. Supported our Church from within and without. Held out for real peace, rather than accept a half-NATO-offering. Offered genuine friendship, not animosity. And perhaps we are. And perhaps that is the very point that your Chief, and NATO, are yet to understand. They talk about it, but we live it. As is the Orthodox way."

"It's poetic, I'll give you that."

"Thank you."

"And encouraging."

"Yes."

"And uncertain."

He laughs to himself. "You know, that's what Nikolai and Dmitry say about you. You may be the only one who truly understands the Russian soul."

Clemmie smiles wistfully, returns her cup to the table and makes for the door. She pauses at the threshold. They share a nod of professional respect. "Don't stop trying. To secure that peace."

"We won't, Clemency. Whatever it takes." He turns away to face the garden. "Even, in the end, if we have to fight you for it."

Chapter Forty-Two

Clemmie and the Chief walk along the waterfront together. A sharp wind whips up the sea in the distance, topping the waves with white foam and sending a sequence of rainbow sprays into the sky. Between her stick and his emphysema, they make slow progress.

"And Stig?"

"I've lost him this time. For good."

"Yes, well, at least for good."

They pause to watch a young child and his father careering along the pebble beach with a kite in tow, trying to achieve lift-off.

"Last I heard, he was off with the younger priest, Father Lev, on some mercy mission. Africa, I think."

"He has good transferable skills I suppose. They're lucky to have him."

"Louise is solid though. I can build around her. If you anticipate there will be a need."

The bright plastic kite suddenly catches the wind and soars high above them with its tell-tale flutter. "They need protecting. Whether they know it or not." He turns to face her. "Regroup and rebuild. I will call."

"Yes sir."

He reaches for his pipe, but Clemmie places her hand on his arm to stop him. "You know, perhaps, Chief, this whole episode has taught us that we need you fit and well. Maybe looking after yourself is as important as protecting everyone else."

He growls, then reluctantly does as suggested and returns the pipe to his pocket. "How very sanctimonious."

Clemmie smiles as she watches him stride off, harrumphing as he goes. "It's all these priests you've been hanging around with. Too worthy by half. Either that or you just want to keep me around so you can come down here and eat the oysters."

She follows him in the direction of the oyster shacks. "Now there's an idea."

END

ABOUT THE AUTHOR

Sven Hughes is a strategic communications professional. He has advised global corporations, prime ministers, presidents, militaries, and royal families. *The Seal of Confession* is his second novel. *Selling St. Christopher* was published, also through Amazon, in 2020. He lives in London with his wife and two children.